MY WEEK WITH THE PRINCE

by

J. Sterling

MY WEEK WITH THE PRINCE

Copyright © 2022 by J. Sterling
All rights reserved.

Edited by:
Jovana Shirley
Unforeseen Editing
www.unforeseenediting.com

Cover Design by:
Michelle Preast
www.Michelle-Preast.com
www.facebook.com/IndieBookCovers

J. STERLING

Print Edition, License Notes

No part of this book combination may be reproduced or transmitted in any form or by any means, electronic or mechanical, including photocopying, recording, or by any information storage and retrieval system without the written permission of the author, except for the use of brief quotations in a book review.

Both stories are a work of fiction. Names, characters, businesses, places, events, and incidents are either the products of the author's imagination or used in a fictitious manner. Any resemblance to actual persons, living or dead, or actual events is purely coincidental.

ISBN-13: 978-1-945042-44-7

Please visit the author's website
www.j-sterling.com
to find out where additional versions may be purchased.

Other Books by J. Sterling

Bitter Rivals – an enemies to lovers romance
Dear Heart, I Hate You
10 Years Later – A Second Chance Romance
In Dreams – a new adult college romance
Chance Encounters – a coming of age story

THE GAME SERIES
The Perfect Game – Book One
The Game Changer – Book Two
The Sweetest Game – Book Three
The Other Game (Dean Carter) – Book Four

THE PLAYBOY SERIAL
Avoiding the Playboy – Episode #1
Resisting the Playboy – Episode #2
Wanting the Playboy – Episode #3

THE CELEBRITY SERIES
Seeing Stars – Madison & Walker
Breaking Stars – Paige & Tatum
Losing Stars – Quinn & Ryson

J. STERLING

THE FISHER BROTHERS SERIES

No Bad Days – a New Adult, Second Chance Romance

Guy Hater – an Emotional Love Story

Adios Pantalones – a Single Mom Romance

Happy Ending

THE BOYS OF BASEBALL

(THE NEXT GENERATION OF FULLTON STATE BASEBALL PLAYERS):

The Ninth Inning – Cole Anders

Behind the Plate – Chance Carter

Safe at First – Mac Davies

FUN FOR THE HOLIDAYS

(A COLLECTION OF STAND-ALONE NOVELS WITH HOLIDAY BASED THEMES)

Kissing my Co-worker

Dumped for Valentine's

My Week with the Prince

Spring's Second Chance

Summer Lovin'

Falling for the Boss

SHE'S DEAD

CELESTE

I CAN'T BELIEVE she's dead.

I mean, I had known that this was coming, but still … the actual loss of her life was like a shock to the system.

I'd basically put my own existence on hold after moving back home to the suburbs of Dallas to be with my mom in her final weeks with cancer. Assuming that it would only be for a little while, I had no problem walking away from the life I'd created in Austin. But what started as a leave of absence at my elementary school teaching job quickly turned into my needing to quit altogether. I had no idea when I'd make it back there, if ever.

Those weeks at home with Mom turned into months, which eventually turned into a year, but truthfully, I never regretted it. Not even during the end, when I watched my once-beautiful mother fade away from being such a bright light into nothing but an empty shell who could barely keep her eyes open. It was heartbreaking to witness, painful on a level that couldn't be described, but I would have hated myself if I hadn't done it. I couldn't have lived with the guilt if I'd let my mom leave this earth alone or with a stranger by her side who was only there because it was their job and we paid them.

Thankfully, my little sister, Tyra, had come home as well near the end.

And now that Mom was gone, all we had was each other. It had always been the three of us for as long as we could remember. Our dad had left when we were just kids and apparently never looked back. He ran off with someone from work. At least, that was the story we'd been told. He got remarried and gave all of his money to his new family, forgetting completely about the one he'd already had, leaving us behind to fend for ourselves.

My mom worked her ass off to take care of two girls by herself and give us a good life.

And she had.

She'd deserved so much better than some bullshit disease eating away at her until it killed her. Mom had deserved to be alive for when her daughters got married and gave her grandbabies. Now, she'd never see any of it.

"I'm so mad," Tyra said angrily, wiping away at the tears that never seemed to stop falling from either one of our eyes.

"I know. Me too," I said, wrapping a protective arm around her and squeezing. "It's not fair."

She exhaled a long breath before turning toward me. "What do we do now?"

It was such a loaded question, one that held far too many answers, options, and responsibility. Neither one of us lived in Dallas anymore. I'd moved to Austin years ago, and Tyra had headed to Houston right after high school. We were both spreading our wings, so to speak, seeking the kind of independence that only moving out could provide. Granted, there was no need to move so many hours away from home, but it'd seemed like the right thing to do at the time.

Now, nothing seemed right.

Everything was discombobulated. Messy. Wrong.

Even though we'd both been here for months, in this house, it was almost like we'd been sleepwalking the whole time. Our bodies were here, but the rest of us wasn't fully present. We had been so focused on Mom, what she needed and how we could help her, that everything else was just a blur of colors and shapes.

I suddenly felt like I was opening my eyes for the first time in over a year, and I could finally see what lay before us. Our childhood home, filled to the gills with years of belongings and memories, all seemed so overwhelming now instead of comforting. Maybe it had only felt that way before because she was still living.

But Mom wasn't here anymore. And we both knew it. Her spirit wasn't sticking around in this old house, waiting for us to decide how to move on and what to do next.

"I'm sure Mom had a will," I said, my head already going into organization mode.

My mother was nothing if not organized. I knew that she would have done whatever she could to make this the easiest on us. She was always putting us first.

Tyra reared her blonde head back. The two of us couldn't have looked more opposite if we'd purposely tried. Me, at five foot eight with dark hair and brown eyes. Her, a tiny, petite thing, barely reaching five foot two, with blonde hair and blue eyes, which we always assumed had come from our absentee father since our mother had brown eyes like mine.

"A will? Who cares about a will, Celeste?" she snapped, and I knew it was because she was emotionally overloaded. We both were.

We'd been holding our feelings in for so long, trying to be strong while Mom was still here with us, that the second she inhaled her last breath, we broke down, exhaustion taking over. That had been a little over a week ago, and we still looked like zombies who had barely survived the apocalypse. Mom hadn't wanted a funeral. That was the one thing she'd made crystal clear and forced me to not only listen to, but repeat back to her. She wanted to be cremated and said that if we felt up to having a *celebration of life*, she'd like that but that we didn't need to feel obligated to do anything.

"I just meant that maybe Mom had some requests she put in there that we don't know about. Like what she wanted us to do with the house."

"You never asked her?"

I shook my head, feeling stupid. I should have thought about these kinds of things, so I could have at least talked to my mom about it all before she died. But I'd been too caught up in simply being present with her that I pushed the painful details off to the side to discuss some other day. Even when she tried to bring it up, I'd force her to stop. It was cowardly and classic avoidance syndrome, but it'd seemed easier at the time to pretend like maybe she'd make some miraculous recovery and I'd never have to think about things like *what to do with the home we grew up in* ever again.

I watched as my sister plopped down in one of the seats at our old kitchen table, the one we'd had since we were kids, her head in her hands as she sobbed. I felt helpless, unable to ease her pain. I had my own. Plus, there was nothing I could say or do to bring back our mom.

And when you sat there and thought about what losing her meant—that we had no parents anymore—it was incredibly lonely and scary, to say the least. I shoved all of that out of my head, refusing to feel sorry for myself any more than necessary.

Tyra sniffed loudly, wiping her nose with the back of her arm before she looked at me, her eyes swollen and red. "Are we supposed to sell it? The house, I mean?"

I shrugged. "I don't know. Neither one of us lives here anymore. But, Tyra, if you want the house, I'll make sure we can keep it, okay?"

I was officially in big-sister mode now. Being four years older wasn't much, but it sometimes felt like a lifetime in terms of experience. Not to mention the fact that even though there was only the two of us, we'd fallen into the societal roles like they had been made for us. Me, the ever-dutiful older sister, who always watched out for Tyra and tried to keep her out of trouble, responsible at all times. And then there was Tyra, the baby of the family, the favorite who could do no wrong even though that was all she ever did.

She pushed the limits while I stayed in bounds.

"Don't you want to keep it?" she asked, almost sounding hopeful.

I'd almost forgotten that Tyra was the more sentimental of us two. She had a really hard time with letting go of things. I only imagined what giving up this house would do to her. I wasn't actually sure she'd survive it, the loss of one more thing.

"I don't know. I haven't really thought about it," I admitted, angry again for not planning better and being more on the ball when I'd had the chance.

"You don't have your apartment in Austin anymore," Tyra added, like I couldn't go back there and get a new one as soon as I left here.

But I knew what she meant. Technically, neither one of us had anywhere to live. We'd both packed up our apartments and broken our respective leases to come back home. And now, we were here … Mom-less.

"I need a drink." Tyra shoved up from the chair, the sound of it scratching against the wood surface, making me shiver.

Mom had hated that sound. She'd always cock her head to one side and narrow her eyes, making sure Tyra knew she disapproved without ever saying a word.

"Crap. Mom would have been giving me *the* look right now," she said as she shuffled toward the kitchen cabinets and started pulling the right one open. "Please tell me you didn't throw out all the good shit."

"I didn't throw out anything. Why would I?" I balked, feeling somewhat disrespected that my sister thought so little of me.

I was never one to throw out alcohol, and one look on that shelf would tell anyone that. Some of it was really old—so old that the liquor wasn't made anymore—but there it sat, in our cabinet, just waiting for its chance. It had to be undrinkable by this point.

I watched as Tyra maneuvered the bottles around, pulling them out one at a time to see what was hidden behind them. Most people had a liquor cabinet, all pretty and on display, but not us. Nope. We just had an old-fashioned cupboard filled with whatever we'd accumulated over the years.

"Thank God," Tyra exclaimed as she pulled out a bottle of Belvedere Vodka.

I wondered where that had come from and how long it had been in there. Belvedere wasn't expensive, but it wasn't necessarily cheap either. Mom didn't usually splurge on the good stuff, as she used to call it.

"There's orange juice and cranberry in the garage," I said, like Tyra didn't know that already.

Was this what someone dying did to your brain? Made you tell people useless information that they already knew, like the fact that there was juice in the garage when she had been the one to pick it out at the grocery store with me just the other day?

I started pacing with no idea of what I was supposed to do—begin packing or go through things and decide what to get rid of. Even if we somehow kept the house, it would still need to be cleaned out.

Mom's room had basically been turned into hospice care. Long gone were the times when we'd sat as kids on her bed as she read to us until we fell asleep. Or nights when we'd run into her room during a storm. Or cried in her arms over boys who had broken our hearts while she told us they'd mean nothing someday.

Now, it was a room filled with memories of pain, medication, tears, and labored breaths. It needed to be aired out and covered up with a fresh coat of paint. My thoughts were racing when I heard my cell phone ringing from somewhere in the house.

"It's in here," Tyra shouted, and I turned to see her waving my phone in her hand as she glanced at it. "No name.

Just a local number," she said as she handed it to me.

I answered tentatively. It was usually a spam caller whenever it was a number I didn't recognize or have programmed in my phone. "Hello?"

"Is this Celeste Finnegan?" the older male–sounding voice asked from across the line, but I wasn't falling that easily.

"Maybe," I said, my response clipped and unfriendly.

"Okay, maybe Miss Celeste Finnegan. This is Charles Edwin. I handled your mother's will. She requested that you come in and meet with me. Not your younger sister, however. Just you."

"Why just me?" I asked.

"Because you're the executor of the will. Can you be at my office anytime soon?"

"I'm not sure," I said, being difficult for no other reason than I felt like it.

"Celeste, this is a very time-sensitive matter. I need to urge you to make time to come in. As soon as possible."

Jeez. Can this guy turn the melodramatics down a notch?

"Fine. I can come right now."

"Sounds great. I have your email address, so I'll have my assistant send you our physical address and any additional details that we require."

The call ended as abruptly as it had started, and I turned to find Tyra staring at me as she mixed together her vodka and cranberry drink. Well, it had to be mostly vodka because the concoction was only tinted light pink, which meant she'd only put a splash of the cranberry in.

"Who was that?"

"Mom's lawyer, I think. He needs me to come into the office and go over the will."

Tyra placed the glass down on top of the counter. "I'll get my things."

"No, Ty," I said, stopping her short. "He asked for just me to come in. Something about being the executor."

She looked perturbed, and I almost thought she was going to argue with me about it, but she reached for her glass again and took a giant gulp without flinching.

"Go then," she said, sending me away with a wave of her hand.

I hurried into my bedroom, grabbed my purse along with my car keys, and headed out the door.

STILL TAKING CARE OF US

♣

CELESTE

I SAT DOWN in the driver's seat of my car and blew out a long breath. Pulling up the email app on my phone, I loaded it, hoping that Mr. Charles Edwin's email had come through. Mom's will was actually something that I was super curious about, but I also wanted to get this over with as soon as possible. The fewer legal things we had to get through, the better.

The email was waiting in my inbox, just like I'd hoped, letting me know the address and to bring a picture ID for identification purposes. I copied and pasted the address into my navigation app and carefully backed out of the driveway. Mr. Edwin's office was only a few minutes away, and even though this was a small town, in my opinion, it wasn't so tiny that everyone knew everyone else. I'd never heard of Charles Edwin before in my life, and I wondered how Mom had found him.

Before I even realized it, I was pulling into a business complex and parking my car in the plainly marked Visitors section. I locked the door with my remote before heading toward the tinted glass doors. I knew from the email that they were on the second floor, but I checked the directory anyway, just to be sure. Suite 231.

I took the stairs one at a time, noticing how quiet the building was. Passing by all of the doors until I reached the right one, I wasn't sure whether I was supposed to knock or walk right in. I grabbed the knob and turned it, pushing the door open to see a quaint lobby and what looked like a check-in area behind a Plexiglas setup.

The woman behind it kindly smiled at me. "Can I help you?" she asked.

I cleared my throat. "I'm here to see Mr. Edwin. I'm Celeste Finnegan," I said, and her face contorted into a mixture of recognition and sadness.

She knew who I was; she had been expecting me. But she also knew why I was there.

"I'm sorry about your mom," she said softly, and I thanked her. "I'll be one moment. Let me tell Mr. Edwin you've arrived."

She disappeared, and I was left alone in this room that was painted too white and decorated too plainly. I guessed that lawyer offices weren't really meant to feel homey. They were all business. And that business was stark, demanding, and cold.

"He's ready for you." She reappeared at a doorway, holding it open for me to walk through. "Right this way," she said as we walked toward the end of the long hall. She peeked her head inside. "Mr. Edwin, Miss Finnegan is here for you."

Charles Edwin was an older man with graying hair and glasses that sat perfectly on his face. He looked pleasant enough even if the business he dealt with was less than. "Hi, Celeste. It's nice to meet you in person."

"Thank you. It's nice to meet you too."

"You didn't know anything about this, did you?" he asked in an almost-jovial manner, like the entire thing was somehow a little comical. Which, I guessed, in a way, it was.

"No. I had no idea," I started to say before adding, "I mean, I assumed that my mom would have a will, but I just thought it would be something written down on a piece of paper that I found at home."

He laughed. "Most likely in crayon, right?"

I smiled in response.

"Your mom wanted everything legal and done by the book. It was the one thing she insisted on."

He talked about her with such affection that I knew they'd been friends.

"You knew her," I said matter-of-factly. It wasn't a question.

Charles nodded once, a small smile playing on his lips. "I worked with her a long time ago."

"At the grocery store?" I wondered in surprise because Charles did not look like the type of guy who would have ever worked in a grocery store.

But it had to have been there because the store was the only place my mom had ever worked. She started in high school one summer and continued working her way up to a manager position and loved every second of it. My mom had always said that most people were in a good mood when they came into the store. And those who weren't usually left her checkout aisle with a smile on their faces instead of a frown.

"I worked in the butcher department over the holidays one year. But we stayed friends on Facebook."

That response made me laugh out loud. My mom had loved her Facebook; she'd had it downloaded on her phone and constantly updated it.

"You knew my dad then?" That one was a question.

He had worked with her briefly at the store as well, as far as I knew.

"I did not. He had already left you guys by the time I started working there. It was just Josie and her two girls."

The smile hadn't left my face, even when I asked about my absent father.

"You know, I tried to get your mom to go out with me. I asked her about twenty times," he mentioned with a laugh.

I tried to picture our life with Charles as our stepdad. He seemed kind enough, but I didn't see it—him with her. Mom had been too carefree, too happy, too whimsical, and

Charles looked like he was wound up a little too tight.

"She never said yes, I take it?"

"Not a chance," he said with a nod, but I'd already known that.

Mom hadn't even dated while Tyra and I were growing up because she said it made her uncomfortable to bring a strange male into a house where two beautiful young girls lived. She'd suggested that it was inviting trouble in, so she put her personal life on hold until the two of us moved out.

"Well, if it makes you feel any better, she never dated anyone while we lived at home."

"I eventually learned that," he said before adding, "Facebook."

My emotions welled up inside me as I heard this man talk with such familiarity about my mom. It was nice. Comforting.

"I guess we should get down to business then. I'm sure you have other things to do," he suggested, and I found myself shrugging.

"Not really. But I'm sure my little sister is probably losing her mind right now, wanting to know what's going on, so—" I explained, and he put up a hand.

"Say no more." Charles grabbed the file folder that was already on his desk and opened it, pulling out papers, one piece at a time. "Okay. This is your mom's last will and testament. Do you want to read it yourself, or do you want me to go over it with you?"

I swallowed hard, wondering what Mom could have needed a legal will for. We never had much of anything. Not that we struggled or really even wanted for things. We just weren't well off.

"Can you go over it with me? I'm afraid if I take it and bring it home, I'll have questions, or I won't know what half of it means."

He smiled, his eyes crinkling around the edges. "Of course."

Charles launched into some legal speak before letting me know that Josie Finnegan had left everything to both Tyra and me equally. We were now proud homeowners and had been for over a year and didn't even know it. The house had been paid off, the property taxes as well as the homeowners insurance paid up for the year.

All of her savings, 401(k), and IRAs were to be divided equally between us girls. As well as the life insurance amount, which he claimed wasn't very much because she'd gotten it after being diagnosed. Wasn't it a shit thing that when you needed insurance to take care of your family because you knew you were going to die, no one wanted to give you any? Like they couldn't fathom actually having to pay out on a claim.

"I didn't even know she had that stuff. The IRAs and 401(k)," I said, surprised.

"Josie worked at that store for almost thirty years. She managed to put away quite a bit of money," he said, pushing a piece of paper in my direction so I could see the dollar amount.

My brain spun inside my head. How had I never even considered that before?

"Is this a joke?" I couldn't even comprehend having that much money, and here it was, being handed over to me for no other reason than the fact that I was still alive and she wasn't.

"She worked a lot of overtime, got holiday pay, double time on Sundays—that kind of thing. She planned for her future and the future of yours and Tyra's as well."

"Tyra's gonna flip," I said without thinking.

Two hundred and fifty thousand dollars each was a lot of money. Not to mention the fact that we got to keep the house, too, and to top it all off, it was paid for.

"Normally, you'd have to go to the store and sign paperwork to get all of this, but they made an exception for your mother. As her trustee, once she became incapacitated from a financial standpoint, I was able to sign everything on your behalf. The money will be wired to your accounts as soon as you fill out this paperwork."

He moved another form in my direction, and I started filling out my account information.

"I don't know Tyra's bank information."

"I figured as much. That's why the whole amount will go to you, and you'll distribute it to her," he said like it was no big deal that five hundred thousand dollars was going to show up in my account one day.

"The money will just go to my bank account?" I asked, still bewildered by all of this news.

"Yes. My partner here at the firm is actually a financial specialist. I know this is a lot of money to come into all at once, so if you girls need any help or financial advice"—he swallowed—"if you want to start investing or anything at all, just let me know, and I'll set you up with him, okay?"

"Okay," I said as I wrote the last two numbers of my bank account on the form, signed it, and slid it back in his direction.

"That's basically it. Her car is paid off, and you can either keep it or sell it. She said she didn't care and figured neither one of you would want it. The title is in the folder." He closed the file back up after carefully putting all of the papers back inside and handed it to me.

"I have one other thing you need to sign," he said. "Just acknowledging that we met and that I went over the will with you and gave you all the contents listed in section two."

"All right," I said, my hand shaking as I grabbed a pen. Turning to section two, I read the list of contents, making sure that I was aware of each thing listed, and signed my name in three places.

I pushed to a stand, shaking Charles's hand and thanking him for all he'd done—for both my mother and for my sister and me.

As I turned to leave, his voice stopped me. "Oh shoot. There's one last thing," he said, holding out a large manila envelope in my direction. "I almost forgot. Your mom would have come back to life just to kill me if I didn't give you this."

I took it gingerly, wondering what it could be when I recognized my mom's handwriting on the front in her favorite green Sharpie.

For My Girls.

"Do you know what this is?" I asked and watched as his eyes started to water before he rubbed at them quickly.

"I do. Sorry, I'm not usually so emotional. Your mom was a wonderful person. I just hate the way it all ended for her," he said, and I felt my own eyes fill with tears.

"Thank you for saying that."

I hated it too. It was total bullshit and not even remotely fair.

"You'll let me know if you need anything or if I can help, right?" he asked as I stepped through his door and into the hallway.

"I will. Thanks again," I said, but we both knew that I wouldn't.

I GUESS WE'RE RICH NOW

CELESTE

I SAT IN my parked car for all of two seconds before I grabbed the envelope, the file folder, my purse, and keys and practically sprinted toward the front porch. Tyra really was going to lose her mind over the money and the house. I hoped she wouldn't do anything stupid, like buy a bunch of new shit she didn't need, but you never could be sure when it came to my little sister.

Sometimes, she was incredibly calm and collected, but other times, she was the most impulsive person I knew. I wouldn't be surprised if she called me in two weeks to tell me she'd bought a bar with the money ... or a club ... or a hair salon or something.

Maybe I should call Charles Edwin back and ask to meet with his advisor.

I stepped into the house, and the screen door slammed closed behind me, alerting Tyra to my presence.

"Celeste?" she yelled, a little crazy, and I wondered how many vodkas with a single splash of cran she'd drunk while I was gone.

"It's me. Where are you?"

"In the kitchen still. I literally haven't moved since you left," she answered and started giggling as I rounded the corner and found her in the exact same place where I'd left her.

"Too much to ask that what's in your hand is the same drink as before?"

"Waaaay too much to ask. You've been gone for, like, an hour. Who takes an hour to drink a drink?"

"Fair enough. You're not drunk though, right?" I asked because the last thing I wanted was to get into Mom's affairs with Tyra in an altered state of mind. I would hate to have to go through all of this again in the morning.

"I'm not drunk," she argued firmly. "Yet. Now, tell me

what Mr. I Have Mom's Will Bigshot Lawyer Dude said."

"Make me one of those first." I decided to join her. "But with way more cranberry. I like mine an actual red color, thanks."

"Lightweight," she whispered under her breath, and I smiled as I watched her fill my glass almost to the top with the juice before adding the vodka.

"Smart-ass," I mock complained but took a healthy sip when she slid it to me. "Oh, this is good."

She bent over in a curtsy before grabbing her glass and giving a nod toward the table. We both sat down, staring at each other, and I could tell that she was a little nervous, or anxious, or something.

She took another healthy gulp of her drink. "You can tell me now. I'm prepared."

It struck me then that Tyra might be thinking that we had been left with nothing, desolate and forced to give up the house.

"Mom really took care of us, Ty," I started before all of the emotions began pouring out of me in the form of tears.

"What do you mean? How so?" She leaned against the table, her eyes locking in on mine and holding.

"She left us the house. It's all paid off. Her car too. And she had a bunch of money saved that we're supposed to split."

I waited for her to ask me how much money, figuring it was the next logical question, but she didn't.

She leaned back in her chair, reached for her drink, and downed it. "We get to keep the house?" was all she asked when she finally spoke, her voice shaking, the tears spilling down her cheeks.

I hadn't realized until that moment how much this house truly meant to her. I'd thought I understood, but seeing her like this really brought it all home.

"She did so much for us." Tyra wiped at her cheeks.

"She did everything for us," I agreed.

Our mom really had. She put her life on hold until we both moved out and started our own lives. She ended up getting sick soon after but never told either of us. I'd like to think it was because she figured she'd kick cancer's ass and none of us would ever be the wiser. But life didn't follow the plans we made for it, and she had been forced to tell us because the cancer was consuming her, piece by piece.

"There's one more thing," I said, and Tyra pulled herself

together momentarily to shoot me a questioning look.

"What else could there possibly be?"

"She left us this." I reached for the manila envelope and slid it across the table toward her.

"What is this?" she asked before spotting the familiar handwriting the same way I had at the lawyer's office. "Can I open it?" Tyra was already working at the sticky glue on the back, trying to get it undone before I even answered.

She gasped and covered her mouth with one hand.

"What is it?" I asked, wanting to know everything.

"It's a letter." She started dumping out the contents of the envelope onto the top of the table. "And tickets?"

My head was spinning, and I wasn't sure if it was all the emotions, the vodka, or a combination of the two.

"Read it. Read the letter," I urged, and she picked it up and started unfolding it.

Then, she read the words out loud.

My sweet daughters,

We always talked about going to new places, didn't we? Having grand adventures where no one knew anything about us, except for what we told them. It always sounded so exciting, and to be honest, I was planning on making it happen. A special trip with my girls.

I'm sorry we didn't get the chance. But just because my life is over, it doesn't mean that yours is. We all know that your lives are just beginning. There are so many firsts you still get to have. So, Celeste, Tyra, GO LIVE. You've not been doing it for far too long, taking care of me. And while I appreciate that more than you'll ever know, it's time for you both to do something for yourself.

I know it must be so hard and painful for you to watch me wither away, but I've loved having you around. Is that selfish? Probably.

Which is why I'm unselfishly—ha—sending you both to Ireland. You know I'll be there in spirit, following you around. Heck, I'm probably already there now, waiting for you to show up. Tickets are here along with your itinerary. It's all planned out. Everything is paid for. There's nothing more you need to do for me. Except this one last thing. Live. Live with all your heart. Start in our homeland.

I miss you more than you'll ever know.

But don't forget—I'll be watching. Don't break all the Irish hearts while you're there.

xxx,

Mom

"What?" I dragged out the word. Just when I'd thought I couldn't stomach another iota of shock, my body squeezed more in. "Read it again. Read the letter again."

"No. You read it again." She tossed it toward me and grabbed what I assumed were the plane tickets and whatever else had been in the envelope. "Silently. Read it silently, Celeste. We're going to freaking Ireland!"

I read the letter five more times until I had it practically memorized. When I looked back down at the table, Tyra had shoved the itinerary in front of my face, and instead of feeling sad, I was starting to feel excited.

"Celeste?" Tyra said my name softly.

"Yeah?"

"We leave in three days," she said, and my jaw fell open as my heart started racing.

"Three days?" I asked, suddenly feeling stressed before

an eerie calm came over me, and then I knew my mom was here with me, telling me it would all be okay.

"I'm going to pack." Her chair squeaked against the wood floor as she shoved it back and disappeared down the hall.

I realized that I never even told her how much money we each had now, but it could wait. The Finnegan sisters were going to Ireland.

IT COULD BE WORSE

CELESTE

MOM REALLY HAD planned for it all. We flew in first class with seats that reclined all the way down and basically turned into a bed. A bed on an airplane! I thought Tyra was going to camp out with her eye mask and never leave.

"This is the greatest thing ever," she said during the flight as she sipped on a cocktail and watched a movie on her own TV. "I don't think I can fly coach ever again."

I almost told her that she probably wouldn't have to if she didn't want to, but something stopped me. I wasn't sure what or why, but I still hadn't let her in on the amount of money we were currently in possession of, and she never asked me about it again.

The entire amount had hit my bank account this morning, right before we got on the flight, and I almost started choking when I saw the number on my phone screen. I'd played it cool, closing the app before Tyra could look over my shoulder and see it and properly freak the eff out.

I figured that I'd deal with all of the specifics of the money, transferring her half to her once we got back home to the States. Right now, I wanted us to do our best to enjoy being in another country, all thanks to Mom.

The plane landed with a jerk, hitting the runway harder than I was used to, but Tyra didn't even budge. She was sound asleep, earplugs in her ears, that damn sleeping mask over her eyes. I reached across my massive seat/bed to touch her and could barely reach. I poked her leg with my finger and kept doing it until she stirred, slowly pulling the mask off of her eyes and blinking up at me.

"What do you want?" she asked with a whine as she popped out her earplugs.

"We're here," I said, a sudden grin taking over my face.

We are in freaking Ireland!

"We are?" She sat up straighter and started stretching her arms over her head. "What time is it?"

I shrugged. "I think it's, like, ten in the morning."

"I'm so glad I slept. Maybe I won't have jet lag."

That had been the plan. To sleep overnight so that when we finally landed here, we would feel somewhat normal, so we could try to acclimate to the time difference without losing a whole day. I'd read a bunch of tips and tricks for international flights online before we left. One of them had said to force ourselves to stay awake until at least seven at night, if possible, no matter how tired we got. I wasn't sure I was up for the challenge, but I planned on giving it my all.

I yawned, and Tyra tsked at me.

"Nope. You'd better have slept on the flight."

"I did. Just not as much as you."

We exited the plane and read the signs, thankful that they were in English as we navigated our way through long corridors and into customs.

"What do we do next?"

"The itinerary says that someone will be waiting to drive us to our destination. They'll probably be waiting in baggage claim the way they do back home," I said, hoping I was right.

After getting through customs, which took five hundred thousand years, we didn't have to wait long for our bags. Another perk of first class was, they came sailing down the chute before everyone else's. I dragged my suitcase behind me, the wheels catching every now and then as I scanned the people waiting around in the common area, searching for whoever could be our mysterious ride.

Tyra leaned toward me and whispered, "There," as she pointed in the distance.

A guy, who looked to be way too handsome for this early in the morning, stood, holding our names on a handwritten sign. The writing was messy, but there was no denying that he was waiting for us.

"Dibs," my little sister said.

As we approached, I could tell he was definitely closer to my age than he was hers.

"Dibs, my ass," I whispered under my breath but knew that she heard me. "Good God, Ty. If all the men in Ireland look like him, we might never leave," I said with a laugh as we continued to get closer to whatever this gorgeous specimen of a man was made of.

He was tall, dark, and handsome. Classically so. With a five o'clock shadow that lined his face and accented his sharp features. It had been far too long since I'd even thought about a guy, but the second his green eyes locked on to mine, I thought my knees might give out.

My breath caught in my chest, and I found myself at a loss for words instead of being full of them, like normal.

"Celeste and Tyra?" he asked, talking so quickly that it was hard to decipher. His accent was also … odd-sounding. Not quite solely Irish, but like it was mixed with something else entirely.

Apparently, I had turned into a dialect expert on the flight over.

I nodded in response to his question as Tyra wasted no time in cozying up next to him in some attempt to claim the dibs she'd said moments ago. He shot me a look I couldn't decipher, but the chills it sent down my spine couldn't be denied. He gave me a smirk, and I swore my heart sputtered inside my chest.

"I'm Patrick. I'll be taking ye to the inn." His voice was deep and sexy.

And even though it was a little hard to understand what

the hell he was saying, I decided that I didn't care. If this man wanted to talk to me all night long, reading out his grocery list, I'd listen.

My voice was still lost somewhere deep inside my body. Every time I opened my mouth to speak or say something in response, no sound came out.

"Did ye have a grand flight? Do ye need to use the jacks?"

That dang accent, so thick and almost muddled but still sexy as hell, coming out of that mouth. That mouth …

Tyra stopped walking and gave him a funny look, breaking me from my self-imposed trance. "What did you just say?"

"Yeah, did you ask if we needed to use the jacks?"

Tyra and I both looked at each other, grins on both of our faces. I guessed I'd found my voice after all.

What the hell is a jacks?

"Sorry, I meant, the loo. I mean, the restroom. We have a wee bit of a drive, and it's pissing down out there. Would hate to have to stop on the way back if we didn't have to."

I couldn't help but laugh. I assumed that *pissing down* meant that it was raining, but I didn't remember seeing any rain from the airplane window.

"It's raining?" I asked.

"Ah yeah." He nodded. "Just started when I arrived to fetch ya."

We followed Patrick outside and toward the parking structure where I assumed his car was waiting to take us wherever we were going—and not to be murdered and our bodies dumped in Ireland where no one would know we were missing or ever come to find us.

When we reached a gray Audi, the trunk popped open, and Patrick took both of our suitcases and placed them inside like they weighed nothing when Tyra and I had both struggled to lift them ourselves.

"We'll both sit in the back," I whispered toward my little sister, knowing all too well that she had planned on sitting up front, next to Patrick. I was having none of her shenanigans right now.

We piled into the car, Patrick sitting in front of me—on the wrong side of the car. Then, I remembered that they did that over here—drove on the wrong side of the road and sat on the wrong side of the car.

"Isn't it hard to drive on the wrong side of the road?"

Tyra asked, her voice serious, and Patrick chuckled.

"It's not the wrong side for me, love," he said, and I swore she swooned at the use of the nickname as she punched me in the thigh.

I was instantly jealous, which was absolutely insane, but there I was, seething that he'd called her love. If I had to spend this whole trip being a third wheel to some love affair, I was going to ... I didn't know what I was going to do, but it wouldn't be pretty.

Patrick paid for the parking and quickly navigated us away from the airport and toward the large metropolis in the distance. Dublin.

"So," I started to say as Patrick's eyes met mine in the rearview mirror, "your accent."

The sides of his eyes crinkled, and I knew he must have been grinning.

"It's a bit fecked, yeah?"

"I guess you can say that." I laughed at the word. "It just doesn't sound completely Irish."

Tyra smacked my leg again. "Why would you say that?" she chastised me before leaning forward, stretching her seat belt out as far as it would let her. "I think it's hot. And it sounds perfectly Irish to me."

I rolled my eyes. I couldn't help it.

"Your sister's right though. I was raised in England. I've only been in Ireland for about six years. So, my accent's a bit of a mash between the two."

"Well, I think it's lovely," Tyra added before sitting back in her seat again, and I refocused my attention on whatever I could see out the window and through the rain.

Everything was so big and bustling, and while it was definitely charming in its own way, it wasn't at all what I had expected when we arrived. I had no idea why I'd simply assumed that Dublin would be some tiny, idyllic town with nothing but cobbled streets, where everyone knew everyone else, but it wasn't like that at all. Minus the cobblestone streets. I definitely saw some of those.

But Dublin was huge. Massive actually. And busy. Crowded. And as cool as the buildings were, I found myself feeling grateful that we weren't staying there. For whatever reason, I didn't want to be surrounded by the hustle and bustle of everyday life that I could experience back home. I wanted to feel like I was in another country, not like I'd never left my own.

"So, where are we going exactly?" I asked even though the name of the town was on the Word document my mom had provided.

"We're technically going to Kilkenny," he answered like I had any idea what that meant or where that was.

I hadn't even checked a map before we left on our trip, too exhausted and overwhelmed from everything in general.

"How far is that from here?" Tyra already sounded impatient. "I'm just tired of sitting," she explained further, and I nodded in understanding. I was tired of sitting still too.

"About an hour and a half's drive. Feel free to take a nap," he suggested, and we both laughed, shouting over each other.

"I've slept enough," Tyra said.

"I don't want to miss seeing anything," I added as I stared out the window at the rolling landscape passing us by.

Our drive continued, us on one of the smallest roads I'd ever seen, as a river appeared out of nowhere before snaking away out of view again. And every so often, hidden by overgrown grasses and trees, I saw what looked to be remains of old castles or churches—I couldn't be sure which. The stonework, even in its decaying stage, was breathtaking. It rivaled something I'd only ever seen in movies before, but it was here, and it was real. Ireland was magical. That was all there was to it.

After being in the car for almost two hours—we'd gotten stuck behind a man pulling a cart for a while—Patrick navigated his Audi onto a dirt-like road, and before I knew it, we were passing by a gray cobblestone building with deep red shutters lining each window. It was downright charming and unlike anything I'd ever seen before.

"Is this where we're staying?" Tyra piped up, seemingly as excited as I was.

A sign that read *The Prince's Inn* hung from a black iron arm, announcing the name.

"Yep. Home sweet home." Patrick's accent worked itself through my bones once more.

"The Prince's Inn," I said, saying the name out loud. "You live here?"

"Aye, I do. I actually own the place," he clarified.

"You own the inn? And you picked us up?" I asked through my surprise.

Most owners back in the States would have hired

someone else to do the picking up.

"Full service, dear."

Dear. No one under sixty had ever called me dear before. But I liked it. A little too much.

And now, I understood how Tyra had felt when he referred to her as *love*. I wanted Patrick to call me *dear* every single time he spoke to me … which I hoped was a lot.

AMERICANS

♣

PATRICK

I'D MET PLENTY of American women before. Especially after that show *Outlander*, or whatever it was called, got popular over in the States. I knew that the series took place in Scotland, but American women were on the prowl for something hot and foreign. And that hunt took them to Ireland as well. I'd been propositioned more times than I cared to admit. Not that it wasn't flattering, but I'd been dealing with women trying to bed me my whole fecking life.

It wasn't something I really enjoyed.

So, I had less than zero expectations when I showed up

at the airport today. Why would I? Tyra and Celeste were just another pair of clients coming here for God knew what. A good time? A quick lay? An Irish fling? It was always the same story—they came here, met some locals, drank our beer, and then went back home to America and never looked back.

I always hoped that if they did return, they'd stay at my inn again. That was the purpose of my being an above and beyond host. Return customers. But that was difficult when most were making a once-in-a-lifetime trip. The best I could hope for in those situations was word of mouth and great online reviews.

When had I become such a wanker?

I was busy watching a couple reunite in the airport that I almost missed seeing her. She was atypically beautiful but beautiful nonetheless. Her long, dark hair needed a brushing, and she looked tired, but it was more than just the flight over. There was a sadness in her eyes that I recognized instantly because I had it too. In mine.

And even though the blonde one was bouncy and friendly and a little too flirty, I was drawn toward the other. There was a heaviness that weighed on her shoulders, no matter how hard she tried to hide it. She was burdened with loss. It was crazy, the way I picked it out of a crowd now that I'd experienced it myself.

The second my eyes locked on to hers, I fought the urge to take her in my arms and save her from the pain she was carrying. But I knew that she needed to walk through it on her own. It was the only way through. And hell yes, I was making a boatload of assumptions right now, but I sensed that my intuition was right on the money.

I found out the one I wanted was called Celeste.

The one I wanted? What the feck?

I could already tell that staying away from her was going to be a challenge. Being tempted by strangers wasn't my usual MO, but everything about her was different. Or maybe it was my fecking savior complex. Seeing people in pain tended to hurt me, and for some reason, seeing Celeste in pain felt like being gutted with a rusty blade.

This girl was going to be the death of me.

☘

ONCE WE GOT to the inn, I showed them to their room. Yes,

they could have found it themselves, but I wasn't ready to let her out of my sight yet. I'd never forget the way they both gasped in pleasure at seeing the space when I opened the door for them.

"Oh my God, this is so cute," Tyra said as she bounced from bed to bed before settling on one of the three singles.

"I'm glad ye like it."

Celeste faced me. "I don't know what I was expecting, but it wasn't this."

"What do you mean?" I asked, intrigued. I wanted in her head, her thought process, her pants.

"Um, well, the building looks old," she said before her eyes grew twice in size. "No offense, I mean. It just looks …" She paused as she searched for the right, non-offensive word to say even though I wasn't offended in the least. "Aged?"

I laughed. "That it is."

"But this room is so light and modern."

I grinned. "I updated it a few years ago to keep up with clientele. Most of ye ladies don't want a dank, run-down room," I said, my accent coming out in a mixture of my two worlds that even I could hear it. Sometimes, my brain got stuck, trying to pick a word, Irish and English mashing together.

"It's really beautiful," she said.

I felt pride in the work that my best mate and I had done. We'd remodeled the rooms with women in mind and made all the adjustments on feedback I'd acquired over the years.

Even when the rooms had been antiquated, they'd still booked out. But mostly to locals within Ireland and a few travelers from the UK. I knew that was because they knew who I was and were trying to bed me. Everyone wanted to win the heart of a prince. Even if he'd renounced his right to the throne and walked away from all aspects of said monarchy with his head held high.

"The pub has really good food and drinks. You don't even need to leave the property for a good time," I said, and Tyra giggled.

"We already knew that much."

I smiled at her but wanted to make my intentions clear—I had no interest in her. "I think you might like Blaire," I said, and the grin died on her face.

"Blaire?"

"He's my best worker and my best mate," I explained,

and her smile reappeared.

"Oh, Blaire's a guy?" She wagged her eyebrows, and I decided that, yes, Blaire and she would get along swimmingly. "Well, maybe the four of us could do dinner together?"

Celeste cleared her throat. "I'm sure Patrick doesn't have time for that. He is the owner after all."

I took a step toward her. "Because I'm the owner, I can make time for whatever I want. I'd love to have dinner with you."

Her cheeks reddened as she looked from my eyes toward her feet. I wanted to tell her not to be shy or coy with me, to let down her guard and let me in so I could keep her safe forever, but I kept the words in my throat. There was no sense coming on that strong even though the thoughts marinated inside of my bones. She looked skittish, and if I'd scared her off already, I'd regret it.

"Dinner would be nice," Celeste said.

"But only if you bring Blaire," Tyra added.

"Six o'clock," I said, and both girls started choking on their laughs.

"Did you say sex?" Tyra teased, but I knew that my

saying *six* sounded like sex to most Americans.

"Ye know what I meant. Do ye think you'll still be awake?" I knew how brutal the jet lag could be even if you'd slept on the flight over.

"I'm up for the challenge," Tyra said before adding, "I'll keep her up."

"If ye don't, I will," I said with a wink before dropping two keys on top of their table and heading out the door before I said or did anything else stupid.

I searched high and low for Blaire, so I could let him know that he had plans tonight. Hopefully, he didn't already have some of his own because I was going to pull the bloke card and make him cancel to be my wingman, as the Americans liked to call it. I finally found him in the stables. I should have looked there first. Blaire loved the horses.

"There ye are," I said, and he turned around like I'd startled him, a brush in his hand.

"I was just brushing Bessy."

"I can see that." I pulled up a footstool and sat down.

He focused his eyes on me, sensing that something was up. "What is it?"

"I need you to go to dinner with me tonight."

"Why would I go to dinner with you?" He dropped the brush to his side and gave me a crazed look.

" 'Cause we're going with two guests of the inn."

"Two guests of this inn?" He emphasized, knowing how rare me even suggesting that was.

I nodded.

"Are these guests women?"

I nodded again.

"Good-lookin'?"

Another nod, and he started howling with laughter.

"What are ye laughing at?"

He kept fecking giggling like a schoolgirl. "You tell her you're a prince?"

I reared my head back. "No. Why would I tell her that?"

"American girls eat that shit up. I'd get a shirt made and wear it everywhere, every day," he said, and I knew that he was serious.

He'd told me that a hundred times before. Blaire would have used his birthright to get as much pussy as humanly possible. But that was because he hadn't grown up in the life. Everything looked inviting when you were on the outside, looking in.

"Everyone here already knows I'm a prince."

"But she doesn't."

"She won't care," I said matter-of-factly, like I knew Celeste's innermost thoughts and desires when I had no clue. At least, not yet.

"How can you be so sure?"

I shrugged. "Just am. So, you'll come tonight?"

"Of course I will. But you'd better not be giving me the ugly one," he said, and I rolled my eyes. "And don't get mad when I let it slip that you're a real-life prince."

"Try not to," I warned but knew it was in vain.

Blaire would do and say whatever suited Blaire's needs in the moment.

"You know I can't keep that quiet when I'm hammered."

"Try not to get hammered tonight then," I said, making a mental note to tell the bar not to overserve him.

Blaire had a big heart, but he had an even bigger mouth.

"No promises, bloke."

Inviting him tonight might have been a big mistake. I guessed I'd find out.

DINNER DATE

PATRICK

I WAS BLOODY nervous. It was absolutely fecking ridiculous for me to be feeling that way, but here I was, standing in front of my bathroom mirror, wanting to change my outfit for the tenth time, like a girl. There was no logical reason for my nerves, but they swam inside me anyway with no signs of letting up anytime soon.

Celeste's sad eyes flashed in my mind, and I wanted to know why they'd looked that way. I wanted to know every single thing about her. *Why did she come here? Does she have a boyfriend back home?*

No. Hell no. I do not want to know the answer to that

question.

There was a quick knock on my door before it flew open, and Blaire walked through.

"You ready?" he asked before looking me up and down.

We basically matched, both wearing jeans and dark jumpers.

"We look like twins, arsehole."

He offered me a shrug, like he couldn't care less. "So?"

"Go change," I demanded, but he looked at me like I was insane.

"No."

"Yes."

"No."

I took a step toward him, pretending to be threatening when he knew damn well I'd never hit him. "Go fecking change."

"If I leave this room, I'm going straight to the girls' room to fetch 'em."

My temper started to flare. The idea of Blaire going to get Celeste and casting his eyes on her before I got to had me seeing red.

"Fine. Let's go," I growled.

He spun in a circle, pretending to model for me as he ran his hand down his chest. "I can wear this then?"

Shaking my head, I headed toward the door without looking back or answering. I knew Blaire was following me—I could hear his Shrek-like footsteps stomping behind me.

"Are we meeting them at the pub or picking them up?"

"This isn't a date," I snapped even though it sure as hell felt like one.

"So, we're meeting them at the pub then?"

"Yes."

"Hope they didn't pass out instead," he said in a teasing tone, but I'd just been thinking the exact same thought.

Their reservation was only for five nights, so we didn't have much time. I wondered at first if they would be leaving The Prince's Inn and heading somewhere else in Ireland, but then I remembered that we were booked to return them to the airport. Their trip was short. At least, it was shorter than most.

We walked through the corridors of my building before reaching the front door. I pushed it open and stepped into the evening air. It was chilly but typical for this time of year.

"Is that them?" Blaire pointed toward the two women about to step through the pub's doors.

"How'd you figure?" I asked because he was right. It was them, but how the hell had he known that?

"They look American." He shrugged, and I shook my head but couldn't disagree.

They did look American—in their high-waisted jeans and tight tops. If Celeste turned around right now and caught me staring at her arse I'd have no excuse to offer.

Blaire sped up. "They look bang-on," he said, "at least from the back."

"Keep yer arse away from the dark-haired one, ye hear?"

He grinned so wide that I thought his cheeks might split. "What if she likes me better than you?"

"She won't."

"She might," he argued back as the sound of music wafted through the air. "How old are they anyway?" he asked, and I realized that I had no idea, so I shrugged.

Someone always seemed to be playing or singing at the pub. It was an Irish way of life. I walked through the open double wooden doors and was greeted by everyone immediately. It wasn't because I was a prince either, but because I owned the place.

Blaire's eyes scanned the dark space, searching for the girls. I saw Tyra waving at us before he did and tapped his shoulder as I headed in their direction. My eyes crashed into Celeste's and held. I wasn't sure why I couldn't seem to look away from her, but here I was again, making things uncomfortable with my *lingering for way too long* eye contact.

When we reached their table, the girls scooted in tighter together. I sat in the open seat next to Celeste, and Blaire moved in next to Tyra. She gave me a small smile, and I knew she approved.

"You did good," Celeste whispered toward me. "My sister's a huge flirt."

"So's he," I said. "Everyone loves the dimples," I added because it was all I'd heard since hanging out with Blaire. How cute he was. How his dimples were to die for.

"He's just her type," Celeste said.

"I figured he might be."

"What about my type?" she asked, catching me by surprise.

For some reason, I hadn't taken her as the forward type.

"That's why I'm here. It's me for you or no one, sweetheart."

She bit her bottom lip, her face pinching together. "I think I can deal with that."

She was flirting. And I was turned on.

"Good. Couldn't bear to see ye hooking up with anyone else in my town," I admitted before thinking better of it.

Her face showed her shock clearly before she reined it back, pretending to be completely unfazed.

"Oh, really? And why's that?" She leaned toward me, her hand suddenly on my thigh. A little lower, and she'd be touching my cock, all hard and ready for her.

I shrugged slightly. "Couldn't say. Just know it to be true."

"How old are you guys?" She narrowed her eyes at me and waited for my response.

"I'm twenty-seven. Blaire's twenty-five. Ye?" I asked, holding my breath.

"Twenty-five," she said, and I felt myself relax.

Thank God.

"And yer sister there?"

"She's twenty-one," she answered before leaning back, Tyra tugging on her arm.

I looked at Blaire, who gave me a thumbs-up before our server appeared, carrying a tray of four shots of whiskey.

"I figured you'd start with these, yeah?" She asked as she placed a shot in front of each one of us.

"Looks great. Thanks."

"What is it?" Celeste asked.

"Some of our finest Irish whiskey," I said proudly, like I'd made it myself when I hadn't.

"Do American girls drink whiskey?" Blaire asked, a little cocky, and Tyra grabbed her glass and downed it in one gulp. "Guess that answers that."

Tyra frowned. "Shit. That was strong."

"Not meant to be taken like a shot, love," Blaire said before sipping at his slowly, as if to teach her.

The two had taken drinks before we even gave a cheers.

I held my glass toward Celeste. "*Sláinte*," I said, and she repeated the toast before taking a tentative sip.

"I heard you have good beer here," Tyra added, and Blaire's face lit up.

"The best. I'll fetch us some pints."

"Whatever you say. I can't understand half of it anyway." She nodded and watched him hop out of the booth and saunter away. "He is so delicious. Can I keep him?" she asked as she turned toward me. "I want him."

I started laughing. "He's all yours. He's a handful though. Don't say I didn't warn ye."

"Yeah"—she stuck out her tongue—"not sure I even remotely care."

"She's the handful," Celeste said, thumbing toward her sister.

"So, listen," I interrupted, "I thought I'd introduce ye to some local fare. It might not be what you're used to back in the States, but ye can't leave Ireland without trying at least some of it, okay?"

Celeste looked nervous. Maybe she didn't eat red meat. A lot of American women didn't, and I hadn't even thought to ask.

"Do ye eat meat?"

"Oh, yeah, I do. I'm not really an adventurous eater," she explained.

Suddenly, Blaire was back, balancing four pints of Guinness in his hands.

"This is beer?" Tyra asked, cocking her head at him.

"You know it is. You're teasin'," Blaire said, and she started giggling.

"It's Guinness, yes?"

"Aye," he said before scanning the table. "What'd I miss? You two look awful serious over there."

"I was telling them that I picked our food for tonight without thinking," I said, and Celeste put her hand on my shoulder.

She looked at her sister. "We promised we'd try new things while we were here. So, we're up for it."

"If ye don't like it, I'll get ye some chips and a burger instead."

"Chips are fries, right?" she asked, her eyes pulled together in confusion.

"Yeah."

"Deal."

She stuck her hand out, and I took it and gave it a firm shake before pretending like the energy that zipped through my entire body hadn't just happened.

Touching her was like playing with fire. And I was ready to get burned.

SO ... IRELAND'S FUN

CELESTE

THE PUB WAS adorable and exactly how I'd imagined it—all dark wood and old, carved fixtures. There was even a guy with a guitar strumming and occasionally singing in the background. Maybe he was the next Ed Sheeran? Hell, maybe Ed Sheeran came here sometimes to sing. I should have asked Patrick, but didn't want to come off as some sort of stalker fan.

Everyone seemed so happy here, like they didn't have a care in the world. And maybe they didn't. Maybe living in Ireland was as blissful as it seemed. Although, to be honest, it was a little cold. The air was wet, but that was also why everything was so beautifully green. Couldn't have one without the other.

When Patrick noticed that I'd been babying my beer, he asked me if I wanted something lighter instead of the "meal" that Guinness was. I thanked him for reading my mind and was grateful when he returned with something delicious and drinkable, by my standards.

He introduced us to soda bread, telling us that it was made a hundred different ways but the inn's way was his favorite. It had a hint of honey, and I had to stop myself from inhaling the entire loaf. We also had Irish stew and boiled bacon and cabbage. I devoured the stew but could only stomach a few bites of the rest.

"Not your cup of tea?" Patrick asked as he finished up every last bit of food on his plate.

"The flavor is"—I paused, thinking about how to word it without being offensive—"not what I'm used to."

"Do ye like fish?"

My face lit up in an instant. "I love seafood."

"Good to know."

"Is it a thing here?"

He nodded vigorously. "Aye. Salmon, cod, oysters, and

shellfish."

"Fish and chips?"

"Yes."

"Do you serve it here?"

"Of course," he said with a smile.

"How long have you owned the inn?"

"I bought it a few years back. Right after I moved here," he explained.

But I could tell he was holding something back. I had no idea what it was, but there was something behind his eyes.

"Can I ask ye something?"

I nodded, taking another sip of my beer. "Of course."

"What brought ye and Tyra here?"

A lump quickly formed in my throat as memories of my mom slammed into me. The reason we were here in the first place. "Our mom booked the trip for us." I pointed toward Tyra, who was practically sitting in Blaire's lap while they fed each other bites of food.

"I remember now. She set it all up with me over email but mentioned that she couldn't travel. Is that still the case?" He shifted his position, angling his body more toward mine while I spoke over the now-dancing crowd and louder music.

"Yeah. It's still the case," I said, using his word choice as I started to get a little choked up and overwhelmed. "Did she say anything else?"

He shook his head. "Not really. Just that she was planning this surprise trip for the both of ye and was sorry she wouldn't get to come."

I sucked in an audible breath, making a sound I couldn't take back. Patrick put his hand on my arm, and my heart rate elevated with his touch and calmed me at the same time.

"She died," I blurted out before I could take it back.

His face twisted in pain. Or maybe it was pity. I hated that it might be the latter.

"Don't feel sorry for us." I sucked in a breath and regained my strength.

He shook his head. "I don't. I mean, I do. Of course I do. Ye lost your mum. It's a terrible thing to lose your mum. I would know."

My breath caught in my throat, my chest aching. He knew. Maybe that was why I'd felt so drawn to him right away—in more than just the way he looked anyway. We shared a common bond, a loss that most people were blessed not to know until far later in life.

"What happened to your mom? Was she sick?" I asked, wrongfully assuming that everyone had lost their parents because of some life-eating disease.

"No," he said with a small smile that held so many emotions that I couldn't read them all. "She wasn't sick. She was full of life. Beautiful. Funny. A really good person."

His eyes started to glisten, and I hated that I was upsetting him.

"You don't have to talk about it. I'm sorry. I shouldn't have asked." I tried to get him to stop, but he put his hand on my thigh and squeezed.

"It's okay. I like to talk about her life. I just hate to think about her death," he said, and my heart stopped.

"God," I breathed out. "That's so relatable." I hadn't had the time to think about it like that yet, but I decided to file that sentence away inside me somewhere, so I could always remember it.

"It was a car accident. Slippery roads. Driving too fast. She and my brother were killed," he explained.

I instantly looked over at Tyra, who was in her own

Blaire-filled world. I couldn't imagine what losing her would feel like. *Devastated* seemed too simple a word.

"I'm so sorry, Patrick. I can't imagine how hard that must have been. How much that must have hurt."

I could tell that scenes were replaying in his mind, the same way that they did in mine. It wasn't something that could be stopped—the memories. They were powerful things.

"How long ago did it happen?"

"Six years now," he said, and my heart ached.

"Does it get easier?"

"No," he answered quickly. "It just gets different."

I nodded my head as if what he'd said made complete sense. He knew that my loss was still fresh, still new, so he graced me by continuing to explain his perspective further.

"At first, it's almost unbearable, ye know? The pain and the loss. Ye think about all the things she won't be around for. She'll miss your wedding, meeting the love of your life and your kids. But at some point, ye stop dwelling on those things, and you'll only think about them every so often instead of every single waking moment."

I fought back the tears because I was still in those

moments, those thoughts, the depths of all that she'd miss out on when it came to Tyra and me. I was still mad that she wouldn't get to see us get married or meet her grandbabies.

"The loss becomes a part of ye instead of something ye carry around. It no longer lives outside of your body, like this tangible thing ye could reach out and hold and show to someone. At some point, ye start to coexist with it. There is no one without the other. It's just who ye are now. Altered."

My eyes watered, and I wiped the moisture away before it could start falling. He looked shaken up and a little uncomfortable, like he didn't discuss this part of his life often—or ever.

"I'm babbling. Does that even make any sense? Probably not."

"It makes perfect sense. Thank you for sharing that with me," I said before fighting back a yawn.

"Ye must be tired."

"I don't want to be because I'm having such a nice time with you, but I am exhausted," I begrudgingly admitted. Even the adrenaline coursing through my veins wasn't enough to keep me up.

He nodded, seemingly hating that I was cutting our

night short, the same way I was. "Let me show ye around tomorrow?" he asked softly, unassuming, like he wasn't at all sure I'd say yes.

"Tyra too?"

He laughed. "Tyra too. I'll bring Blaire with me—unless they're sick of each other by morning."

We both turned to look at them, and they were attached at the lips.

"How long have they been making out?"

"I have no idea," he said with an exasperated look on his face as we watched Blaire get up from the table and walk toward the bathroom.

Tyra was suddenly in my face, her silly expression making me laugh.

"You good?" I asked her, and she smiled.

"I'm going home with Blaire tonight," she said matter-of-factly before looking at Patrick. "I can, right? It's okay if I go to his room and bone the Irish out of him and into me?"

Patrick let out a gruff laugh. "I've already told ye, he's yours for the taking."

She clapped her hands together and made an excited sound. "This is already the best trip ever, and we just got here."

I smiled in response to her words as Blaire walked back to the table before leaning in to give Tyra another public kiss, the two of them completely enraptured in one another and forgetting that the rest of us were even here.

"Do you guys do this often?" I asked, suddenly wondering if this was their thing.

They had the perfect setup for it, working at an inn filled with short-term tourists. The ideal vacation fling, weeklong romance, or whatever you wanted to call it.

Who could blame them for hooking up with all the random women who came to stay? I imagined them charming the pants off of every single woman who visited ... *literally*.

Patrick looked like I'd struck him. Then, he looked solemn. "No. It didn't even occur to me that ye might think that. But it does look that way. No, Celeste, I never do this. Blaire has once or twice before but not often. It's a rule I have for myself. No hooking up with the clientele."

"But I'm clientele," I added, dying for him to tell me that I was good enough to be his exception.

"Technically, your mum's my client," he said with a grin before adding, "I told ye that there's something about ye. I meant what I said."

I wanted to argue, push him for more, or say something logical in response to stop this nonsense, but all I could hear was the sound of my heart beating in my ears. Patrick made me feel alive. He made me hopeful. He was like a paintbrush, slowly adding splashes of color in a world that had turned to black and white the day my mom got sick.

"I never do this. Have dinner with the tourists. Or offer to take them sightseeing." He took my hand in his and ran his thumb across the top.

I believed him. Whether or not that made me a fool, only time would tell.

"I can't seem to let ye go," he said so sincerely that there was no room for doubt.

I held his hand a little tighter in response to his words. "Don't then."

His eyes pulled together. "Don't what?"

"Let me go."

"I don't plan on it." He brought my hand up to his lips and pressed a kiss there.

It was only then that I glanced around the pub for a split second and noticed the shocked look on people's faces.

They had been watching us. For how long, I had no idea. But their expressions told me that Patrick wasn't lying to me. If he did this sort of thing all the time, no one would be surprised or pay us any attention. Patrick and his antics would be old hat, so to speak. The fact that they were observing our every move—or at least, *his* every move—told me all I needed to know.

Patrick was one of the good ones. And I wanted him.

I WANT THIS WOMAN

♣

PATRICK

I WALKED CELESTE to her room and fought the urge to lean down and kiss her before telling her good night. It was too soon, right? Too soon to want her the way that I did.

But nothing inside of me was currently feeling that way. Being around her was comfortable in a way I couldn't begin to describe.

And my past had forced me to keep most people at a distance. It wasn't until I'd moved to Ireland and met Blaire that I started realizing how truly abnormal the way I'd been raised was. When you'd been surrounded by a certain kind of person for your entire life, you had no comprehension that everyone wasn't that way. Of course, I could look back at it now and see how sheltered I'd been.

Celeste walked into her room, holding the door with her hand. "Tyra will be safe with Blaire, right?" she asked, as if the idea of being concerned for her safety hadn't occurred to her until that moment.

"Yes. He's flirty and fun. But he's not dangerous. And he's not mean. She'll have a good time," I tried to reassure her.

Blaire was harmless, and I was willing to put my neck on the line for him.

"Okay. I mean, she's old enough to make her own decisions, but"—she paused before looking down at her feet—"they just met."

"We just met," I said instantly.

"But we're not spending the night together," she argued, her cheeks starting to blush.

I swallowed hard. "No, we're not."

My words came out funny, in an almost-bitter-like tone, which wasn't how I'd meant them at all.

"You're jealous."

I almost laughed at the idea, but she wasn't wrong. I was

jealous. Jealous that Blaire could do whatever he wanted without giving it another thought. Because if I could be as free as he was, without any regard to the potential consequences, I'd have Celeste underneath me already, making her moan, writhe, and scream my name all night long. And then I'd turn around and do it all over again tomorrow.

"I think you're right," I agreed, and her lips turned into a frown.

"You like my little sister?" she asked, and I started shaking my head so fast that I thought I might give myself a headache.

I reached for her cheek and cupped it. "No. No, ye know I don't. I like ye." I wanted to be very clear with her.

"Then, why are you jealous?"

Celeste wasn't a stupid woman, but she was pressing me. She wanted to hear me say things that I had no business saying out loud, let alone even thinking.

"Because Blaire can do whatever he wants. He isn't the owner of the inn. And he doesn't have the father that I do," I started to say but stopped myself quickly. I'd almost slipped up and told her who my dad was.

She was confused by my last statement. It was written

all over her face, but bless her heart for not asking me to go there or pushing me for more information.

"In case you were wondering, I'm dying to be kissed by you."

"Can't have ye die on me, sweetheart," I said before stepping toward her and taking her lips with mine.

I was cautious at first, moving so slowly that it was almost torturous. But when her mouth opened and her tongue found mine, a switch flipped. I turned ravenous, afraid I might not ever be able to get enough as I savored her every taste, craving more.

"Patrick," she breathed out, my name a whisper on her lips that I wanted to hear over and over again until it killed me.

Pulling away enough to separate our lips, I opened my eyes to look into hers. "Are you okay?"

"I changed my mind," she said, and I took a full two steps back. "No, no. The other way."

"The other way?" I asked, trying to read her thoughts but failing.

"I had convinced myself that it would be okay if I slept with you tomorrow. Like somehow adding a day would make a difference. But I don't want to wait. I don't want to waste any moments when I could be spending them with you."

She didn't have to ask me twice or say another word. She'd given me permission, and I intended to take her up on it.

Pushing her through the door with my body, I slammed it shut behind us before turning to lock it. "In case little sister comes home before we're ready," I said, and Celeste smiled in response before licking her lips.

She was going to be the death of me—I was certain of it. But what a way to go.

Before another thought entered my head, her lips were back on mine, her tongue making its way inside. Her hands gripped my back, sliding underneath my shirt as her fingers dug into my flesh. I tried to stop myself from moaning but couldn't. It slipped out, and the grin on her face only grew wider.

"I didn't even do anything," she said.

"It's your touch. When your skin is on mine, it makes me feel like a live wire," I admitted, and it only spurred her on.

She grabbed the bottom of my sweater and tugged, pulling it off of my body before gasping and running her fingertips down my chest and abs. "Good God. You are unreal."

She leaned forward, her lips pressing against the warmth of my skin, making chills spread over my body. The feel of her on me, touching me, kissing me, was enough to make me come undone, but I did my best to hold back and let her take control. For now. Her hands were on my pants, working at the button and the zipper before pulling them down.

"My shoes, sweetheart. Let me get them off," I said before she started giggling.

"Whatever. Leave 'em on for all I care," she said, and it was my turn to laugh.

"There will not be a single thing between us when I make love to ye. Not socks. Definitely not shoes. Nothing," I said as I sat down on one of the beds and untied my boots before kicking them off. Celeste started to do the same with hers, and I stopped her. "I'll get those," I instructed.

Her eyes widened as she looked at me, her hands dropping to her sides. "Okay," she agreed as I made my way to her body sitting on the edge of the other bed.

Dropping to my knees, clad in only my boxers, I untied her laces and gently pulled her shoes off before removing her socks. I kissed her calves before sliding up her legs, my fingers already gripping the insides of her thighs. I pushed to a stand and extended both hands toward her. She took them, and I pulled her up before I removed her clothing, all while peppering her body with kisses. When I pulled down her panties and placed a kiss on her clit, her knees almost buckled from the contact, and it turned me on even more. My dick was so hard, just from being near her.

"You're beautiful. So fecking beautiful," I said, my breath catching in my throat as I took her in.

Her body was curvy, her tits small but perfectly round, and her hips looked like they had been made for me to hold on to. I wanted to memorize every inch of her skin.

"You need to get naked," she demanded, pointing at my boxers, which were still on.

I did as she'd asked, her eyes focused on my dick as it sprang free.

"I can't believe I'm doing this."

"Do ye not want to? Have ye changed your mind?"

Celeste sat down on the edge of the bed, her head almost

perfectly lined up with the head of my dick but I tried not to think about that.

"No. I just can't believe how sexy you are. Do you even realize it? You look like you should be on the cover of a magazine." She reached out to run her fingers down my stomach once more, not stopping until she reached my dick, her hand cupping it as she moved to stroke it.

"I can't think when ye touch me like that," I admitted, and she started to work faster before leaning forward.

Oh God, was she going to put me in her mouth?

"Jesus," I sputtered the instant her mouth hit my dick.

She started sucking slow, her hand still stroking the base of my dick, and I thought my brain might explode in my head and I'd short-circuit.

She moaned in pleasure, seemingly liking the way I felt in her mouth as her sucking and speed both increased.

"Sweetheart," I moaned, "I'm not going to last if ye keep doing that." I hated to admit it, but it was true.

Ladies, a man is only so strong when his dick is in your mouth. Do eu have any idea how incredibly sexy ye look, taking us in, knowing that in that moment, ye completely own us? It takes a ridiculous amount of willpower not to lose it within seconds. Why do ye think we have to close our eyes and look up at the ceiling? Because watching ye suck us off is one of the most erotic things in existence.

Celeste continued to suck for a few more seconds before she let me go with a pop. "Oh, I like doing that to you."

She wiped at her lips, and I grabbed her body, lifting her up before tossing her on the bed.

Hovering over her, I dropped my mouth to hers, kissing her hard. Our tongues crashed into one another, each one pressing, moving, trying to claim the other. All the while, the sounds coming from our bodies were a soundtrack of pleasure that I'd never unhear as long as I lived.

I moved to her neck, her earlobe, biting and sucking so hard that she shoved me away at one point. Dropping down toward her chest, I took each nipple, one at a time, between my teeth, nibbling lightly before sucking with so much force that she cried out in pleasure, her hands pulling at my hair.

"That mouth," she said breathlessly. "I'm in love with that mouth."

I couldn't stop the smile that formed with her words, spurring me to use it further south. I moved lower and lower, and right before I got to her perfectly pink pussy, I paused and glanced at her. Her brown eyes were wide, watching me with rapt attention, her jaw open as she waited. With a wink, I dived down, my tongue licking at her folds, and she grabbed my shoulders with both hands and squeezed so strongly that I thought she might leave marks. I didn't care.

"Ye taste amazing," I said, meaning it as I continued to eat her out.

She writhed underneath my mouth, my fingers teasing her clit as I fucked her with my tongue. I could have feasted on her pussy all night long, but I had other plans. Like being inside her. I was dying to know how she would feel, wrapped around my cock.

With one last long lick, I pushed to my knees, my dick so hard that it hurt. "Shit," I said, and she looked concerned.

"What?"

"I don't have any condoms with me. I don't carry them around."

"Where are they?"

"Back at my place."

"Hold on," she said before hopping over toward what I

could only assume was her purse and digging through it. "Tyra usually has some," she said, and I felt relieved for whatever reason that it wasn't her purse. She pulled out a strip of condoms, a giant smile on her face as she handed me one.

"Thank God for Tyra," I said before ripping one open and rolling it on.

Celeste moved back into the same position she had just been in and waited. I positioned the head of my dick toward her entrance and pushed in. Even through the condom, I could feel how warm and wet she was for me. It felt amazing, being inside her. I couldn't even speak. Moving in and out, I watched as her eyes opened and then closed before I leaned down to kiss her. I didn't claim her, like I had earlier. This time, I kissed her softly, like she might break if I pushed too hard. I wanted to be gentle with her, loving even.

The sounds she made were going to star in my fantasies for months to come.

"You feel so good," she breathed against my chest, her lips pressing into my skin.

And as her fingernails ran down the length of my back, I realized how well our bodies fit together, all perfectly aligned. There was no awkwardness or having to finagle our body parts around.

"Never stop," she said, and I wanted to assure her that I never would, but I couldn't lie.

"You're so beautiful, Celeste. Ye feel amazing," I confessed as our bodies slapped together and the sweat started to form.

This should have been just a fuck. Or at the very most, sex with no strings. But it felt like something more than either of those things. It felt more like what love might feel like. Or at the very least, the start of it or something like it.

What the hell was I going to do when she left?

A FREAKING PRINCE

♣

CELESTE

I WOKE UP, wrapped in a pair of muscular arms. They were tight around my body, heavy and warm. Memories of last night flooded my brain, and the soreness between my legs crept into my awareness. It had been far too long since I'd allowed a man inside me.

He had been so many things, all wrapped into one—gentle and rough, sweet and dirty. Patrick was unlike any man I'd ever been with before. He knew what he was doing, and he did it all extremely well.

His body started to stir, and I wanted to laugh that we'd woken up at the same time. Of course we had. It was almost as unbelievable as us climaxing together the first time.

"Are you awake, sweetheart?" he whispered against my shoulder, and I turned my body around to face him.

"Uh-huh. How'd you sleep?" I asked.

And he grinned, his dark hair all mussed up from the sex and sweat. He was so attractive.

"Like a log. Ye?"

"I think it was the best sleep I've had in months," I admitted before he stretched his arms above his head and pressed a kiss to my head. "Is it going to be weird now?" I asked, wondering if we were supposed to pretend like this had never happened or what.

"Is what going to be weird?"

"This." I waved a finger between the two of us. "Are you going to avoid me?" I figured the best tactic was to be honest, to come right out and ask so that I knew how to act for the rest of the trip.

"Why would I avoid ye?" He sat up, his green eyes wide. "I want to bury my cock in ye every chance I can," he said, and I busted out laughing.

"Okay, but ..." I tried to figure out my thoughts and how to word them.

"What are ye thinking? What's troubling ye?" He sounded so damn sincere. Like someone I'd been dating for years as opposed to a man I'd just met not even a day ago.

"I don't want to get you in trouble with other customers. And I'm just not sure how you want me to act around other people."

"I'm going to kiss ye in public. I'm going to spend every day with ye until ye leave and break my heart," he said, and I swore my heart started jumping like it was on a trampoline.

"Pretty sure that will be the other way around," I said out loud, but it was the truth.

By the time I left here, I knew I'd be leaving part of my heart with Patrick in Ireland, whether I wanted to or not. It was one of those things that couldn't be helped. Love or lust was funny that way.

A loud knock on the door scared the crap out of me.

"Let me in! Why is the door locked?" Tyra's voice shouted from the hallway.

"Does she sound mad?" I asked Patrick, who was already out of bed, pulling on all his clothes, which was a damn shame, if I was being honest. "You should walk around naked all the time. You'd get more customers."

He jumped back on the bed and kissed me hard. "Ye want everyone else to see me naked?"

I snarled in response, "No. Forget I said that. Stay fully clothed unless you're with me." I suddenly felt possessive over every square inch of that man's delicious body.

"Holy shit, Celeste, wake up! Let me in!"

"I'll get her on my way out. Want to feed the animals with me?"

"You have animals?" I asked.

Patrick, Ireland, and this inn were full of surprises.

"Aye. Meet me downstairs in thirty minutes?" he asked, and I nodded, watching him walk to the door before opening it.

"Final—" Tyra started before stopping short. "Oh. *Oh!* Hi, Patrick. Fancy seeing you here."

"Mornin', Tyra. I trust ye slept well?" he asked in a jovial tone.

"Not much sleeping on our end, Pat. How about you?" She wagged her eyebrows at him before throwing me a look.

"I'm sure your sister will tell ye all about it. See ye in a jiff, sweetheart," he tossed over his shoulder before disappearing.

Tyra slammed the door shut and squealed before running to her bed and hopping on it. "Do you think this is what Mom had in mind?" she asked with a full-on belly laugh. "I know she's watching us right now. Probably super proud of her two girls. Going to Ireland and bagging the hottest guys in the country. Especially you," she said before continuing, "A prince!"

I shook my head and choked out my response, "A what? What are you talking about?"

Tyra's features twisted. "He didn't tell you?"

"Who? Tell me what?"

"Patrick's a prince, Celeste. A real-life prince. Like a Cinderella-loving fairy-tale prince."

"Says who?" I asked with a smile because she had to be pulling my leg.

There was no way that Patrick was a freaking prince.

"Blaire told me. But he told me not to tell you—" She slapped her hand over her mouth. "Oops. I just figured that since he spent the night here, he probably told you."

I was mad. I had no idea why I was so upset, but I was.

"He didn't say anything?"

"No," I answered through clenched teeth as I replayed the night.

Sure, there hadn't really been a perfect time for him to mention that he was a freaking prince, but when was there ever? It wasn't something that fit naturally into a conversation.

"I'm sure he was going to tell you later. You were probably too busy last night."

"Sure," I said, agreeing because it was easier than thinking that maybe he never planned on telling me.

"Ah, don't be mad at him, Celeste." Tyra watched me from the safety of her bed. "Can I tell you about my night?"

I tried to shake off the disappointment I felt that Patrick had kept this secret from me. A secret that I was certain the entire town was aware of. It made me feel stupid, being kept in the dark. I wasn't sure if that was a logical reaction to this or not, but it was still how I felt.

"Tell me about your night." I relented, doing my best to not feel sorry for myself and be happy for Ty.

She went on to give me way too many details about Blaire and how great he was and how much sex they'd had and how many times she'd orgasmed.

"I'm never leaving here," she said once she got to the end of her story.

"Fine," I said with a shrug. "You gonna marry the guy?"

"Ew, what?" Her head reared back like I'd thrown something at her. "I just want to bang him for all of eternity."

"You're not normal."

"I know." She sounded so proud. And most likely, she was. "I need to shower, and then we're meeting the guys for breakfast." She hopped off the bed before turning to face me. "Unless you don't want to anymore."

"No, I want to."

"Thank God. I would hate to have to ditch you for Blaire this whole trip."

She disappeared behind the bathroom door, and I knew that she'd meant it. Tyra would absolutely abandon me for a guy, and I wouldn't even blame her. After the year we'd had—when we'd been surrounded by no one, except each other—I would understand her desire to get lost in some hot Irish guy.

Maybe that's what I'm doing too?

The thought tasted sour in my mouth as I rolled it around. I wasn't doing that at all, and I knew it. But I was still mad at him.

A freaking prince. Prince of what? Of where? What does that even mean?

※

FORTY-TWO MINUTES LATER, we were heading downstairs to meet the guys, like directed. I was purposely late, for no other reason than I wanted to be difficult. Plus, I was trying to think of what to say to him when I saw him, but all my plans flew out the window the second those green eyes met mine and I noticed him standing there, a giant smile on his stupidly perfect face.

"You're a freaking prince?" I shouted.

He instantly looked behind him at Blaire, who threw up his hands and shook his head.

"You knew I'd let it slip," Blaire confessed, not much of a defense at all.

Patrick took a step toward me, his eyes filled with what looked like regret. "Why are ye so angry?"

"I don't know!" I stomped, acting like a crazy girl with a thousand emotions running through her all at once. "I feel like you lied to me, I guess."

"I didn't lie."

"But you didn't tell me."

"There wasn't a right time, sweetheart."

"No." I put up one hand in a stop motion and stepped away from him. "Don't sweet-talk me right now. I can't handle hearing your accent. Were you ever going to tell me?"

That was the question I wanted the answer to the most. Because for whatever reason, it felt like it mattered. If he wasn't going to tell me who he was and where he had come from, what else wasn't he going to mention?

"I don't know," he said honestly, and I started fuming.

"Why not?" I sat down on the wooden bench and put my head between my hands, trying to calm myself.

"Because it doesn't matter," he said, sitting down next to me.

I wanted to scoot away, but I liked his nearness. Our bodies called to each other. Even when I was pissed at him, my body betrayed me.

"How can it not matter?" I asked before looking up and seeing the sign for the inn. "The Prince's Inn. Oh my God. And you own it. And you're a prince. And …" I stuttered, feeling dumb all over again.

"It's a play on words. Wasn't meant to be real, but everyone here already knows I'm a prince. I used to come here with my mum when I was a kid."

Talking about his dead mother was a low blow. He knew there was no way I could stay angry with him when he brought her into the conversation.

"Then, tell me why it doesn't matter. Are you going to be a king? Where are you a prince? How is this a real conversation I'm having right now?"

The very idea of royalty was so foreign to me. Since we didn't have kings or queens in America, the subject had always felt more like a made-up fairy tale than something that was real. The whole thing was … far-fetched, and I had no clue how any of it worked.

"Tell me the truth," I said, needing to hear all of it.

"We'll give you two some time alone. Come on, love," Blaire interrupted before grabbing Tyra's hand and disappearing out of view right as my stomach growled loud enough for us both to hear.

"Ye want to eat first?"

"No. I want to talk first."

He sucked in a breath, his face crestfallen, like he was in trouble. "Okay. I've got two brothers. Well, one now. He's the one who would become king, if it ever got that far. But it won't. I mean, all of my cousins and their children would basically have to die for that to happen," he said, and it hit me in that moment that he was somehow related to the current king and queen.

"How does your family fit in? I mean, how are you related?"

"The king's my uncle. He and my father are brothers."

I nodded in understanding even though I didn't really have a clue what any of it meant. "So, you grew up as a royal? Like, in a castle?"

He laughed, but it felt somewhat hollow. "No, we grew up in what I consider a house, but I think ye might consider it a castle."

This was too weird.

I pushed to a stand and started pacing back and forth, my feet kicking at the small pebbles in the dirt as a million thoughts and questions raced through my head. When Patrick stood up too, he reached for my hands, and looked me in the eyes, it felt like none of it really mattered. I was making a big deal out of nothing, and I had no idea why.

Who cared that he was a prince and hadn't told me? It didn't change the person I had been getting to know or the man that I had given my body to last night. The man who had made me feel like the most beautiful person on the planet. He wasn't wrong when he'd said there wasn't a right time to mention the fact that he was technically royalty. But still … I had one question.

"Why'd you leave?"

He was still holding my hands as he moved us back to the bench and sat back down, his body angling toward mine as he began to speak. "When I was little, we spent a lot of time with my cousins. Our grandmother wanted to make sure that the royal way of life was instilled in our way of thinking. Even though I'd never become king, the pressure to perform and learn and behave in certain ways was still on my shoulders." He let out a breath before continuing, "I hated it. Resented it really. It never made any sense to me, so I was always getting into trouble, acting out. I knew that being king was never my role to fill, so I didn't take any of it seriously. I never wanted to be king anyway."

"Why not?"

"Because it's suffocating, Celeste. Your life is not your own. My uncle and my cousin—the future king—are puppets. They're who they have to be. Who they're supposed to be. They don't get any free will at all. Every decision is made for them. Regardless of what they want. They don't get to think for themselves. They have to follow procedure and rules that are so old that they don't even make sense anymore," he explained, and my heart ached for the strange men I didn't know even though his words resonated with me.

I felt like America did that as well sometimes. Kept fighting for things that had been thought up so long ago that they were no longer relevant in our day and age. They'd made sense at the time, but times had changed.

"You'd never go back there to live?"

"No. When I left, I was forced to give up my title. Which I'm fine with. Truly. I haven't been back, except for my mum's and brother's funeral."

"She died when you were here? In Ireland?"

"Yeah," he said, and I felt the shock rip through me.

For whatever reason, I'd wrongfully assumed that he must have left his hometown after she was killed. Like her death had been the catalyst for him going away in the first place.

"Do you still talk to your dad?"

He didn't even remotely look sad when he answered, "No. We don't speak. He was mad when I left to come here."

Patrick didn't have anyone he considered family anymore. We were more similar than I'd imagined.

"But my mum, she encouraged me to come here. Told me it was all right to go and live my own life. That she wasn't mad, like my dad was," he said with a sad expression. "I'm so grateful I had those moments with her. I would have always wondered otherwise if I had let her down or disappointed her somehow."

"I think she'd have been proud of you." I offered a small smile, feeling as though I understood him even better now. "Look at what you've built." I waved an arm around the property, really seeing it for how spectacular it was.

"I know she'd have loved ye." He leaned toward me,

cupped my face, and kissed me softly. It was an emotional kiss, one filled with pieces of his heart and promises said without any words.

"I wish I could have met her," I spoke against his lips, which were close enough for me to kiss again. "I wish you could have met my mom."

"Me too." He kissed me hard then, our lips pressed against each other, not opening, no tongues, just two mouths connecting like they belonged that way; together.

My stomach grumbled again, and Patrick laughed as he pulled away. "Let's get my girl some food."

His girl.

I definitely liked the sound of that.

THE CLIFFS OF MOHER

☘

PATRICK

THANK GOD CELESTE had understood about my heritage and not walked away from me. I could have fecking killed Blaire for letting it slip before I had the chance to tell her. He could have ruined everything, and I wasn't sure I would have been able to forgive him if that had happened.

This woman had me all twisted up inside, and I wasn't even trying to figure out why.

It had been way too long since my heart had felt anything other than empty. I resigned myself to believing that love wasn't in the cards for me. That I was destined to live my life alone, single, and I told myself that I was okay with that.

I honestly thought that I was.

And then she'd walked through the airport and straight toward me.

I wasn't sure I'd ever be all right again. It was ridiculous to be feeling this way and having these kinds of thoughts already—the logical part of my brain knew that. But it wasn't my brain that was in control right now; it was every other part of me. The parts that had no name. The ones I couldn't explain or reason with or control.

It was all the parts that *felt* without knowing why … they just did.

We walked into the main living room, where breakfast was set up every morning, and found Blaire and Tyra gazing into each other's eyes like two lovesick teenagers. I tossed my phone on top of the table, causing Blaire to startle.

"Oh. Good. You two are okay then?"

"No thanks to ye," I grumbled.

"I'm really sorry about that," he apologized, looking straight at Celeste and not me.

"It's okay." She squeezed my arm. "I'm just glad I

know."

"Me too," I said before kissing her cheek and pulling out a chair for her to sit.

As the four of us ate, I looked at the girls and asked, "Is there anywhere in Ireland that ye want to see? Do you have places ye want to check off a list?"

The girls looked at each other and shrugged before saying, "The Cliffs of Moher?" pronouncing it all wrong, saying *Mo-hair*.

"The Cliffs of Moher," I said, saying I properly as *More*, and they repeated it. "Ye should definitely see them."

"How far are they from here?" Celeste asked.

"About two and a half hours," Blaire said, and I swore Tyra groaned.

"You don't have to come," Celeste said, looking at her sister.

It was crazy how little they looked alike. I wouldn't have guessed they were related at all, as they were so completely opposite.

"Are they magical?" she asked, looking directly at Blaire, who nodded.

"They're a must-see, love," he responded, and the smile

took up her whole face as she dived toward him and kissed him again.

I looked away. They were ridiculous. "Anywhere else?"

"Seeing some castles would be cool," Tyra said with a laugh. "Not 'cause you're a prince. But we don't have castles in America."

I knew exactly where to take them and what to show them. I planned on making Celeste fall so in love with Ireland that maybe she wouldn't want to leave. Or at the very least, she'd want to come back.

After we finished eating, I made sure to check in with my manager before telling her that Blaire and I planned to be off the property for most of the day. She ensured me that there were no handyman issues for Blaire that couldn't wait and that I could entrust the place in her capable hands. She'd been working for me for three years, and I trusted her.

I didn't usually leave the inn, except for the occasional airport pickup when I was feeling bored, but that really wasn't my job. I had a young'un who did that for me. But for whatever reason, the day Tyra and Celeste had arrived, I'd decided to go myself.

"We need to visit Bessy before we go," Blaire said, and

I nodded as Tyra frowned.

"Who's Bessy?"

"You'll see," Blaire teased before taking off toward the stable, making Tyra chase him.

I looked at Celeste, who looked peaceful, relaxed, and happy. "Bessy's our horse."

Her face lit up. "You have horses?"

"We have all kinds of animals," I said, pointing at the stable and the barn in the distance. "Do ye ride?"

"I mean, I haven't in years, but I always loved it." Her brown eyes twinkled, and I knew I'd take her riding before she left.

My heart literally ached inside my chest every time I thought about her getting on a plane and going back to America, so I pushed the thoughts from my head and focused on the here and now.

Right now, she was with me.

Tomorrow, she still would be too.

That had to be enough … even though I knew it never would be.

After brushing the horses and visiting the sheep, I insisted that we get a move on. The cliffs were over a two-hour drive away, but that could change with the weather or the roads.

"Did ye bring jumpers? The cliffs can be rotten."

"Jumpers? Rotten?" Celeste looked at me like I'd grown three heads.

"Jackets. Do you have jackets? It's going to be wet and probably windy there."

The girls opened their mouths in understanding.

"Be right back," they said in unison as they rushed off, most likely heading to their room to grab jumpers … er, jackets.

They reappeared quickly, carrying warmer clothes in their arms. Once we were all piled in the car, I made sure to point out all the local sights—Kilkenny Castle, St. Canice's Cathedral, and Rothe House and Garden. Each one, even though I didn't stop, elicited gasps from both of the girls. When the sights hadn't been so familiar to me, I used to feel the same way as they did—in awe of their beauty. Now, it seemed, I took them for granted a bit.

The drive was long, the road winding, and there were

ruins of what used to stand tall scattered all across the land. I'd grown so used to seeing these things that I looked past them as well. Seeing Ireland for the first time through Celeste's eyes was exhilarating and exciting.

"Are those gravestones?" She pointed in the distance, where old, dilapidated stones stood.

"I believe so."

"It's so beautiful here. Even the parts that aren't standing anymore. There's so much history." Her eyes continued to scan the roads, looking everywhere all at once.

I glanced in the rearview mirror to see Blaire and Tyra attached at the mouths once more. "Can ye two stop lobbing the gob for five seconds?"

They broke apart instantly, and Tyra stuck her tongue out at me. "It's not my fault you're driving, so you can't make out with my sister."

She wasn't wrong. Maybe I'd be doing the same thing with Celeste if someone else was driving.

"We're almost there."

We finally pulled into the parking lot for the cliffs and stepped out into the chilly air.

"It's cold out." I had grabbed a warmer jumper for

Celeste, just in case she needed it.

The four of us stood outside the car before we started walking. I reached for Celeste's hand and held it tight.

"What's that?"

I looked at where she was pointing. "It's the visitor center."

"Is it built inside the hill?" Tyra asked, her tone of voice filled with shock.

"Yeah. The entire thing is technically underground. It's incredible," I said, remembering the first time I'd visited it.

I led us toward the stairs that would take us up to the cliffs, practically holding my breath in anticipation.

The Cliffs of Moher were one thing to see online or in pictures, but in person, it was something else completely. I knew that Celeste was going to lose her mind when she saw their actual scale and grandeur.

"It's freezing," she said, and I held her body tight against mine as we walked in unison.

"Holy shit," Tyra said as soon as we got to the top of the stairs, the full view of the cliffs in front of us.

"Wow," Celeste breathed out, letting go of my hand and I fought the instinct to take it back. "They're unreal."

I stood there, staring at her, thinking the exact same thing.

She plopped down then, right in the dirt and the sand, wrapping her arms around her knees as she stared out into the oblivion of the sheer rocks and the ocean crashing below. I had no idea what kind of thoughts were rolling around in her head, but I knew that if she wanted to share them with me, she would. I refused to push. She'd just lost her mum after all.

Tyra dropped down next to her and put her head on Celeste's shoulder before whispering something into her ear. Celeste looked at her before throwing an arm around her sister and squeezing her. They sat like that, the two of them, and I pulled out my phone and snapped a few pictures to send to her later. That reminded me that I didn't have her phone number. There was no way I'd be letting her leave here without getting it.

I glanced over at Blaire, who must have been thinking the same thing I was because he was in a crouched position, taking pictures of the girls from the back, the cliffs in front of them. He gave me a head nod before coming over.

"They're something else, aren't they?" he asked, and I

wasn't entirely sure if he meant the girls or the cliffs.

When he turned his phone so I could see one of the photos he'd taken, I understood that he was talking about them. Our two American sisters.

"They are," I agreed, and he looked almost solemn.

"I'm going to miss her," he said, and I fought back my shock.

I hadn't been lying when I told Celeste that Blaire didn't hook up with the tourists, but I had left out the fact that he'd hooked up with half the damn town. Blaire was the quintessential bachelor, never falling for anyone, except maybe my horse, Bessy.

"Are ye now?"

"Aye. She's so much fun, Patrick. Like a breath of fresh air. Unlike any other girl here in Ireland." He waved his hand around all the people surrounding us. "No offense to the Irish lasses. But you must know what I mean."

"I do. Want to know the truth?" I asked, unable to believe that I was going to admit this to him. He nodded, and I leaned a little closer to him, the wind whipping between us. "I can't even bear to think about her leaving in a couple days. It tears me up inside."

He smacked my shoulder good and hard. "I thought I was the only one feeling that way."

"Ye too?"

"Aye. How can we trick them into staying?" he asked, and I started laughing.

Not because his suggestion was silly, but because I'd already been thinking the exact same thing.

How could we keep these girls here with us forever?

IRELAND IS INSPIRING

♣

CELESTE

I SAT ON the ground in front of the famous Cliffs of Moher with my sister next to me and a man I'd never expected to meet somewhere behind me. I was convinced in that moment that Ireland was magical. There was no other explanation for the way it made me feel. It was like the land gave me peace and comfort—two things I'd struggled to find at home in America, even before my mom got sick.

There was so much competition back home, like we were running a never-ending race to see who could achieve what the fastest and then never being satisfied with the results or always yearning for more. It was stressful, just being alive sometimes.

"You okay?" Tyra asked.

I turned to look into her blue eyes, which were a little glassy, and I knew she was thinking about Mom.

"I'm good. You?"

"Yeah." She smiled, but it didn't reach her eyes. "I wish Mom could have seen this. Pictures do not do this place justice."

I let out a laugh. "Not even remotely. Look at the size of these cliffs. They're sheer all the way to the ocean. And they go on forever."

"I know. I wonder how many people die here each year," she said morbidly. "Babe," she screamed, no doubt looking for Blaire.

He appeared instantly. "Yes, love?"

"How many people fall off these cliffs and die?"

He started laughing. "I have no idea. None? Why? You want to be the first?"

She swatted at his arms, which were wrapping around her in jest. "No. I want to know. I'm looking it up when we get back," she said, and he disappeared again.

"Mom's here," I said, breathing out and closing my

eyes, wishing it were true. "I know she's with us." I started thinking about her letter and the things she'd said about coming along with us. I was sure when she'd planned this for us, she'd never thought that both her daughters would have some sort of Irish love affair in the process.

"She wouldn't miss out on this for anything. Plus, what else would she be doing?"

I shrugged because I had no idea what people did once they died. Maybe her spirit was teaching in a classroom, or dancing in a ballroom, or falling in love somewhere in the clouds up there. Wherever she was, I just hoped she was happy. And I was grateful that she was no longer in pain.

"I'm going to take some pictures," Tyra said before pushing herself up and reaching for my hand to help me do the same.

"I've got her," Patrick's thick voice suggested, and before I knew it, he was guiding me up and into the warmth of his body.

I looked up into his eyes, mesmerized by the green before he closed them, his lips meeting mine. My mouth opened in response, our tongues touching softly, slowly, erotically.

When we broke the kiss, I swore I felt my heart expand inside my chest. It grew in his presence. I turned around, my back pressing against his front as he held me in his arms and we stared at the magnificence in front of us.

"There's magic here," I said as I stared at the ocean below, the waves crashing without abandon into the rock walls. "I can feel it."

Patrick turned me around, so I was facing him. "Ye think so?"

"I know so. I think folklore and fairy tales started in Ireland."

"I think they end here too." He ran his fingers through my hair and breathed me in.

"Are there any stories about the cliffs?"

He gave me a crooked grin. "What kind of stories?"

"Myths? Legends? Mermaids? Fairies?" I asked with a grin of my own.

He grabbed my shoulders and turned me back around so that I was facing the cliffs as he spoke into my ear, his breath warm even though it gave me chills. "There's a legend about a fisherman and a mermaid," he started to say, and I gave an excited sound. "It's not really a happy story, sweetheart," he added, and I felt myself pouting.

"Tell me anyway," I demanded.

"One day, a fisherman spotted a mermaid. They struck up a conversation, and he noticed that she had a magic cloak. He wanted it. During their conversation, he stole her cloak and ran up the hill."

"Jerk," I breathed out, and Patrick laughed, his chest rumbling against my back.

"She couldn't go back to the ocean without it, so she followed him up the hill to his home. But she couldn't find the cloak anywhere. He'd hidden it."

"I hope he drowned," I said without thinking, but selfish people made me bitter.

"She eventually married him. They had kids, but she never forgot about her cloak. One day, when the man was out fishing, she found it and returned to the sea, never to come back again."

I waited for him to say something more, but he stopped.

"That's it? That's not even romantic," I complained.

"It's the only story I know. Actually, there is another, but it's not happy either now that I think about it."

"I don't want to hear it."

"Okay."

"Will you guys take a picture of us?" Tyra's voice soared through the wind and into my ears before I pulled away from Patrick and reached for her phone before I started snapping pictures of them without warning.

"Oh, these are gorgeous. You're going to love them," I said even though the wind was blowing and her hair was all over the place. It spoke the truth.

Blaire turned to kiss her, and I continued taking pictures, knowing that Tyra would love to have these once we were back home.

Ugh.

The second I even thought the word *home*, my heart felt like it had dropped right out of my chest and onto the dirt I'd just been sitting in. I didn't want to leave.

"Your turn," Tyra said with a grin as she pushed both me and Patrick toward the edge.

"Do ye want a picture?" he asked.

"I want a thousand," I said without thinking, and he smiled so big that it warmed my entire body.

"Me too."

We stood there, wrapped in each other's arms, as Tyra

bossed us around, attempting to pose us. A giant gust of wind came out of nowhere, and I lost my balance, tripping on a rock and almost falling to the ground, but Patrick's arms were around my body, stopping me from hitting anything, except him.

I glanced behind me, noticing how close I was to the edge, my heart pounding inside my chest. "I think you might have just saved my life."

"Then, ye owe me," he said before kissing my nose.

He moved to my lips, and I lost myself in that kiss, forgetting that Tyra was taking pictures until I opened my eyes and saw her moving around us in a circle to get photos from all angles.

I wanted to be embarrassed, but I was actually grateful. This trip had already been the most memorable vacation of my life. I hoped I never forgot a moment of it.

"This is really pretty and all, but I'm freezing, you guys," Tyra said, her hands shaking as she tucked her phone into her back pocket.

I could have stayed out there all day, taking in the smell of the water and studying the way it seemed to lash out at the rocks, wanting it to fight back. My imagination sparked to life, and I stared into the abyss, looking desperately for a mermaid's tail or something else equally as magical. I knew it was out there, if only I searched hard enough.

"We should go, sweetheart. We have a bit of a drive back," Patrick suggested.

I begrudgingly agreed. To be honest, I couldn't even feel my fingertips anymore.

When we got back into the car, Tyra AirDropped me the pictures she'd taken, and I stared at them in awe. The scenery was one thing, but the looks on both my and Patrick's faces ... well, it looked like we had been a couple our whole lives. We looked so comfortable with one another, and I guessed, in essence, we were. At least, I was.

"What are those?" He glanced over before focusing on the tiny, winding road.

"Pictures of us," I said, unable to hide the smile on my face.

"Are they nice?"

"They're perfect."

"Will ye send them to me?" he asked, almost sounding uncertain, like I might deny him or tell him no.

"Of course," I said before realizing that we didn't have

each other's phone numbers, or social media handles, or anything. "I guess I need your digits, huh?"

"Digits?" he repeated the term with a smirk.

"Yeah. Phone number. I have that app where you can talk, video, and text people in other countries for free."

His eyebrows rose in question. "Oh, do ye, now? Who else are ye talking to in other countries?" He sounded jealous as he gripped the steering wheel so tight that his knuckles turned white.

"I have a few girlfriends in Australia. I mostly talk to them."

He visibly relaxed. He had genuinely been worried that I was speaking to random guys in other places.

Instead of letting that thought simmer in his mind, I put a stop to it. "I don't have a boyfriend. In America or anywhere else. In case I didn't make that abundantly clear last night."

I was not the type of girl who cheated or messed around with guys when she had someone in her heart. It wasn't in my nature.

"I don't have a girlfriend either," he said, his grip on the steering wheel lessening, the color coming back into his fingers.

"I should hope not," I said, suddenly feeling stupid for not having asked before I let him inside me. "So, you're not betrothed to some princess somewhere?"

Blaire busted out laughing from the backseat, and I turned around to glare at him.

"Go away. Kiss my sister or something. Pretend you're not here."

"I never thought about that, Patrick," Blaire's voice boomed inside the car. "Are you betrothed? Do you have to marry a princess? Will you turn into a frog if you don't kiss a lass?"

"Not that I'm aware of, feck you very much," Patrick growled.

The rest of the ride went on much that way. We joked and listened to traditional Irish music—not Ed Sheeran, who was only from Ireland. Each time I asked Patrick to stop so I could hop out of the car to take pictures, he obliged me willingly, never once complaining. There was so much to see ... so much history left in crumbles all around us. I swore that if I closed my eyes hard enough, I might wake up in another time when I reopened them. Not that I wanted to be anywhere else.

How was I ever going to forget this trip or this man?

THE COUNTDOWN IS ON

PATRICK

I COULDN'T STOP thinking about the fact that she'd be gone soon. Next week, she wouldn't be in my car. I wouldn't be able to glance in the passenger seat and see her sitting there, smiling at me. Knowing that Blaire felt the same way helped me feel a little less psychotic about the whole thing.

Because honestly, it was crazy.

Then again, there wasn't anything wrong with me falling for someone after a few days if Blaire did it too, right? Maybe it was them, the girls. They were witches who had come and cast a spell on us. We were at their mercy, no say in the matter, no choice in how fast and hard our hearts had fallen.

I started laughing, the music from the pub thankfully drowning it out.

"Is it always like this?" Celeste asked with a giant smile on her face.

"Every night."

It really was. Someone always had a guitar at the ready to pluck or an entire band available to hop onstage at a moment's notice. And the crowd was always willing and waiting to do a jig. I knew that it seemed foreign to Celeste and Tyra, but it wasn't unlike the cowboy bars back in the States, where everyone knew the same dance and how and when to do it.

"I'm fascinated," she whispered into my ear.

I stared at her, taking in her features, memorizing them, even though she'd already sent me the pictures we'd taken together. It had taken everything in me not to make it my screen saver the second it arrived in my gallery.

I wanted to. Like a fecking wanker, I wanted to, but I decided to wait until she left. Then, I'd put it wherever I pleased, and no one would be the wiser. As much as I loved my pub—and trust me, I loved it a lot—I craved being alone with Celeste more.

"I want to spend every minute with ye. Is that selfish? Should I be leaving ye alone?" I asked, hoping like hell she'd tell me no.

"I don't know if it's selfish, but I feel the same way. Thank God Tyra found someone too; otherwise, we'd be having a very different conversation right now," she added seriously.

I'd thanked my lucky stars for that fact many times.

"Want to get out of here?" I asked, and her eyes danced.

"I thought you'd never ask." She turned toward her sister. "We're going to go. Is that okay?"

Tyra grinned. "Yeah. Wait, will you guys be in our room again?"

Celeste shot me a questioning look.

"I'll take ye to my place tonight."

"It's all yours," she said to Tyra.

I stepped out of the booth and extended my hand, knowing she'd take it within seconds of seeing it. Pulling her against me, I danced with her for a few steps before everyone started cheering and making a scene. I shook my head as we walked out of the noisy bar and into the night air.

"Where do you live? I don't even know," she said as I led her toward the main lobby. "Wait, can we stop by the room, so I can get some of my things? Is that weird?"

"Not weird at all."

I waited for her outside of her room while she grabbed whatever it was that she needed. She emerged, almost blushing, carrying a petite overnight bag. It was adorable. I led her toward my place—a small freestanding structure separated from the actual inn but right next to it. The only bad part was that customers sometimes confused my place for the main entrance even though there was no sign above my home. They knocked at all hours of the day and night, apologizing profusely once they realized their mistake.

"Where does Blaire live?"

"Ah, above the stables," I said.

She shook her head, laughing. "Near Bessy?"

"Yeah, his first love," I added. "There's an entire second floor that wasn't being used for anything, except storage. He asked me if he could turn it into an apartment, so he could stay there instead of in one of the inn's rooms. He did all the work himself. It's actually really nice up there."

"That's impressive."

"He is my handyman for a reason."

"I wondered what the heck he did here," she said, and I realized that we had probably never talked about Blaire and his job on the property. "I mean, I just never asked. I've been too caught up in getting to know you."

I stopped walking. "I like ye being caught up in me. I feel the same."

Tilting her head up, I kissed her, my tongue sweeping in and tasting hers before pulling away.

"I know you do," she said, reassuring me, and for some reason, it settled my frantically beating heart.

There was something so calming about being on the same page as someone else. Especially when it came to things as complicated as feelings.

I'd met plenty of American women over the years, but none had been like Celeste. I wasn't sure why, but it seemed like most American women enjoyed playing mind games. They wanted to be chased, never coming right out and saying what they thought. Celeste wasn't like that. Maybe it was the loss of her mum, so fresh and new, that she felt like she had nothing to lose by being honest. Or maybe she had always been this way. All I knew was that it suited me. She suited me.

"My place is just up ahead." I pointed at the stone building lit up by a single porch light.

"I love it already," she said, and I held her tighter, dying to get her naked and underneath me so I could put myself inside of her again.

When we stepped through the threshold, she let out a sweet sounding gasp. "It's so charming."

"Does that mean you think it's small?" I asked, almost offended.

My place was honestly too big for one person. There were rooms and areas that I never even stepped foot in most days.

"What? No." She gave me a crazy look that told me I'd taken her words all wrong. "I love it. It's so pretty." She walked over toward my favorite space in the whole entire house. "This fireplace is stunning. The stone," she gasped as she ran her fingers down the original gray stones that dated back hundreds of years. "It's huge," she said as she stepped inside it and stood up.

I started laughing as I pulled out my phone. "Don't

move," I directed and snapped a few photos of her looking ridiculously adorable, standing inside my fireplace.

It was actually more of a hearth. If I wanted, I could cook over the flame, the way they had back in the olden days. It even had a swinging metal arm that held pots attached to it.

"Can I come out now?"

She ducked down, and I waved her out.

"I've never seen anything like that. Except for maybe in a history book."

"It's my favorite part of the house."

I watched as her eyes narrowed, a sly smile creeping across her face.

"What about your bedroom?"

"It's never had a reason to be my favorite. But I think ye could change that," I said before sweeping her body into my arms and heading down the hall toward the refurbished master.

When I kicked at the door, it swung open harder than I'd meant it to, crashing into the wall before she hopped out of my grasp.

She spun in a circle. "This is the most majestic bedroom

I've ever seen."

I tried to see it through her eyes. The room was abnormally large with a king-size bed and a separate sitting area that held a couch, a chair, and bookshelves filled to the brim. There was a meager fireplace in here as well. But I never used it because I didn't spend much time in my room. There was a massive walk-in closet that had barely anything in it, except my stuff, which honestly wasn't much.

"This. Is. Unreal." She emphasized each word as she said them. "That's it, Patrick. I'm moving in." She laughed, and I swore my heart skipped a damn beat with her words as my mind suddenly envisioned it—her here, living with me, in my home ... *our* home.

"It's all yours, sweetheart," I said, taking a step toward her, my need for her overwhelming everything else. "I need to be inside ye."

"Oh." She sounded a little shocked at my forwardness. "Well, don't let me stop you."

I watched as she walked backward until her legs hit the edge of the bed, and she dropped to sit on it.

I stalked toward her, a man on a mission. A mission to sear myself into her bones, so she could never get rid of me … to become one with her, so we could never be separated as long as we both lived and breathed. Pulling open the nightstand drawer, I reached for a condom, hoping like hell it wasn't expired. Shoving it into my pocket, I looked her deep in the eyes, telling her everything I wanted to say but couldn't. At least, not yet. I poured all the love in my heart into her with just one look and hoped she could *feel* it.

Her hands gripped the back of my neck as she pulled me toward her mouth, and I kissed her like I'd never get to do it again. Like it might be my last time. Like she might disappear if I opened my eyes, and all of this would have been some sort of twisted fantasy that only existed in my head instead of the best version of reality I'd ever lived in.

The taste of her tongue turned me on, and I felt myself grow even harder. Our mouths were fused together, neither one of us willing to pull apart as we tore at each other's clothes, both wanting the other's off. We maneuvered, pulled, and ripped, nails raking across backs, sounds of pleasure coming from both of us. Unfortunately, I had to break the kiss to get her completely naked, but that gave me the chance to worship all of her curves instead.

She moaned each time my lips touched her skin, her hips

bucking as my fingertips traced her body up and down.

"I'll never get tired of being with you," she admitted, and my heart soared.

Yeah, ye heard me right. My heart fucking soared because I was so in it with this woman. This woman I barely knew. This woman who, up until a few nights ago, I'd never even known existed.

But none of that mattered. Because love wasn't always sensible. In all the stories and folklores and tales to be worshipped and adored, love had never once been a thing of sanity. It was all-consuming, rule-breaking, logic-defying. And that was what we all hoped to find someday. A love that broke the mold and made us whole.

My pants were in a heap on the floor, and I reached back into the pocket to pull out the condom and tossed it on the bed. While I was on my knees, I spread her legs with both hands, and her head popped up to look at me, that slack-jawed expression on her face again as she waited for the first lick. Leaning down, never breaking eye contact, I swiped at her length with my tongue and watched as her head rolled back, her eyes closing. I wondered what it felt like for a moment—to have your pussy being eaten—but all those thoughts disappeared when the taste of her hit me and I found myself craving more.

I licked and licked, sucking her clit before playing with it with my fingers. I alternated between licking her pussy with a flat tongue and diving into her hole, my tongue hard and rigid. Everything I did made her moan, scream, and pull my hair. Before I knew it, she was coming all over my tongue, her body jerking softly. When I went to lap up the rest of her, she moved away.

"Oh my God, no. I need a second. Don't touch anything down there," she explained, her voice breathless.

"Don't touch anything?" I teased, my finger lightly tracing her clit before she swatted it.

"Seriously, Patrick. Please. A second."

I decided to obey her. My goddess.

I rose to my feet to remove my boxers before reaching for the condom. Tearing the wrapper, I rolled it on and knew I was fecked. Looking down, I saw there was a rip. "Shit."

"What's the matter?" She leaned up onto her elbows and stared at my cock.

"The condom tore."

"Don't you have more?"

"Aye, but I think they're expired."

She batted her eyelashes at me, her chest still rising and falling. "I'm on the pill. I don't even know why. I just never stopped once I started taking it. And I'm clean, if you're worried."

I hadn't been worried.

"I am too," I said. "Not on the pill. Clean, as you say."

Celeste smiled, and those beautiful brown eyes crinkled at the sides. "Then, get inside me. With nothing between us," she demanded.

And who was I to deny my girl what she'd requested? Making love to her with a condom on had been one thing, but going bare might damn well kill me.

She scooted back further onto the bed, her head resting on a pillow as I hovered above her. My dick didn't even need my help with finding where to go; it practically dived inside of her the second it got near her entrance. I easily slipped inside her. She was still soaked from the orgasm I'd given her. But once I was inside, I wanted to die and live there forever.

Her pussy was hot, and it gripped me like it didn't want me to leave either. There was nothing between us, and we both knew it. It changed things. Made me feel ... *more*. It connected us. I stared deep into her eyes, and she did the same, both of us moving our hips in sync with one another, never breaking eye contact. Something sparked to life in those moments. The air around us felt lit with electricity as I worked myself as deep as I could go.

"Ye feel amazing. I thought ye felt good before, but this is something else entirely," I said.

"You too. I can't believe how different this feels." She worked her hips, holding me in deep and clenching me with her walls.

I held out for as long as I could, moving slow until I couldn't take it anymore. "I have to feck ye hard now, sweetheart."

"God, yes. Fuck me," she said, and I started pounding into her. Each thrust sent her head into the headboard, and before I could ask if she was okay, she begged me for more. "Harder, Patrick. Fuck me harder."

I did. I fecked her hard, using all of my hip strength as I plunged into her faster and faster, still going as deep as she'd allow.

"I love fecking you." I reached for her shoulders, so I

could give her even more, and she cried out in pleasure.

"God, yes. Don't stop. Harder. Faster."

She was a demanding little nymph, and I fecking loved it.

"I'm going to come so fecking hard in ye."

The sound of the bed hitting the wall in perfect time became our anthem. Our bodies slapped together, the sweat dripping as I fecked her even harder as my dick grew, on the verge of release.

"I'm going to come. So fecking hard. So fecking …" The words died in my throat as I groaned and exploded. I filled her with my cum, my dick still thrusting in and out until I drained every last drop of me inside of her.

When I went to pull out, she gripped my shoulders, stopping me. "Don't leave yet."

I fell on top of her, trying not to crush her as we lay there, our bodies literally connected, my head on her tits. Her chest heaved, her breaths quick and labored.

"That was incredible," she exhaled, and I lifted my head to look at her.

"It was," I said, almost at a loss for words as my heart reminded me that she wasn't mine to keep.

Celeste didn't live here, and I would have to let her go soon. I had no idea how I was going to do that. Especially after tonight.

CAN'T BELIEVE I HAVE TO LEAVE

♣

CELESTE

THE NEXT COUPLE of days flew by faster than I'd wanted them to. If there were a way to stop time, I would gladly do it. But life didn't work that way. Patrick offered to take me and Ty to see more of the sights of Ireland, but he had a lot of guests checking in and out, and I knew the idea of being away from the property was actually stressing him out even if he'd never admit it to me. Plus, Tyra and I were both content to hang around the inn, riding the horses, feeding the sheep, and pretending like we lived there.

I'd even helped out at the front desk when the manager

had to step away to handle something for her parents back at their farm. What I figured would be a quick twenty-minute or so coverage turned into me manning the desk and learning the ropes of the check-in procedure for two and a half hours.

I didn't mind though. I'd actually enjoyed it.

Being here, in some strange way, felt like being home. Like I belonged.

When Patrick suggested that Tyra and I go into town and be typical tourists for a while, I said no. The last thing I wanted to do was leave or see anything that didn't include him seeing it with me. For whatever reason, I didn't feel like I was missing out on anything even though I was sure that I was. Thankfully, Tyra felt the same way. We were smitten with our men. From our perspective, they were the best part of Ireland anyway. Not some tourist attraction that everyone had access to.

Mom had told us to live. And in my opinion, there was no better way to live life than through experiences. Sights could be seen any old time. But connections like this, they were rare and had to be taken advantage of. Some might call us pathetic, but those people didn't know Blaire and Patrick.

They weren't like typical American men, hiding their feelings behind all of this made-up bravado and ideas of what a "man" should and shouldn't act like.

No. Patrick willingly admitted how he felt. He wore his heart on his sleeve and made me feel comfortable with doing the same. I'd never been so open and honest with a guy so fast in my life. It was part of what had me falling so hard, so quickly. That level of honesty had been a little uncomfortable at first, but he made it so easy. Mostly because I believed all the things that he said. Patrick's actions matched his words, and he left little room for doubt. I knew how he felt about me because he not only told me, but he also showed me. What took most American guys months to do took Patrick a freaking day. Literally.

So, I sat in the room that Tyra and I were supposed to share but hadn't for even one night, packing up the rest of my things while she did the same.

"I never even slept in this bed," she said with a laugh, "or used the bathroom here."

"I'm aware."

"Don't act like you slept here more than once," she chastised, and I grinned.

"I'm not," I said, trying to be strong when I currently felt anything but.

"Celeste?" My sister's voice sounded off, so I stopped folding my clothes and looked at her.

"Yeah?"

"I don't want to go," she admitted, and I huffed out a breath.

"I know. Me neither."

She plopped down on the bed and wiped at her eyes. "We don't have to, you know. We could stay."

I'd thought the same thing a thousand times in the past few days. How there was nothing pressing forcing us to go back home right this second. But my thoughts always ended the same way ... eventually, we'd have to leave. We didn't live in Ireland. And we'd left so suddenly that there were still a few things I needed to make sure were handled in regard to the house and Mom's affairs. Just to be sure.

"We *could*," I stressed the word before continuing, "but we'd still have to go back home at some point. And it would just make it harder."

"Maybe we'll come back?" she asked, her tone hopeful. "Or they can come see us?"

I laughed at the thought. Not that seeing them again was funny, but I could barely picture Patrick or Blaire in America. I had this sinking feeling that they wouldn't like it there. That all the things that excited people about our country would turn them off.

"I guess we'll see." I still hadn't told Tyra about Mom leaving us money, and it was sort of the perfect time to tell her, but I got nervous that she would become irrational and insist we stay, so I would hold the news inside until we got back home.

There was a soft knock on the door before it turned and opened, and Blaire stepped through the threshold, his hair tucked inside a ball cap.

"You two almost ready to go?" he asked, his eyes rimmed with red, like he'd been upset or maybe even crying.

Tyra launched herself in his arms before wrapping her whole body around him like a BabyBjörn. I watched as his grip on her tightened, his muscular arms flexing. Her body started shaking, and I knew she was crying. I wondered if this was what our mom had hoped for her two girls—to have them leave their hearts in a foreign land.

He kissed her cheek, and I saw it then … his own tears. It made my eyes water in response to seeing them so emotional. I looked away and finished putting my clothes into my suitcase before easily zipping it up. I hadn't bought anything here, like I'd thought I would.

"Patrick's waiting with the car out front," Blaire said, and I nodded in his direction without making eye contact.

This drive to the airport was going to suck.

Blaire wheeled both of our suitcases down the hall and out the door for us. The second I stepped outside and saw that it was raining, I almost started laughing. Even the sky was crying for us. Patrick's green eyes met mine, his expression solemn, and I lost it. I started crying right then and there, bending over at the waist, trying to hide my face. Patrick was there instantly, his strong arms around my middle as he held on to me from behind.

"Don't cry." His voice was strangled as he made a sniffing sound.

I straightened my body and turned around to face him. "Aren't you upset that I'm leaving?" I asked, suddenly feeling stupid around him instead of safe, like I'd felt the rest of the time.

"More than ye know," he said, blinking a few times, and that was when I noticed how moist his eyes were. "I've been thinking of ways to have ye miss your flight all morning," he said, and we both laughed even though we weren't happy.

"We need to go." Blaire's voice filtered into the air.

Patrick grabbed my hand, bringing my knuckles to his lips as he pressed a kiss there. "This is going to break me," he said.

He pulled me toward the passenger side, opened the door for me, and helped me inside. I felt broken already.

Blaire and Tyra were wrapped up in each other in the backseat, neither one of them speaking a word, their foreheads pressed together as they breathed. It was an intimate moment, so I didn't say anything to ruin it.

We drove to the Dublin Airport in silence. Each one of us caught up in our own emotions, having conversations in our heads, talking to our hearts. Patrick held my hand the whole way, always caressing or squeezing and never stopping. Every so often, our eyes would meet and hold before he had to look away and focus back on the road again.

There was so much that was spoken in those moments

of quiet. So much that was said without words. Apparently, we didn't need them.

When he parked the car and shut off the engine, he reached across the seat and pulled me into his arms. It was awkward, but I didn't care. I held on to him for dear life too.

Blaire and Tyra exited the car. I only knew because I heard the doors opening and then slamming, and Patrick moved to press a button that popped the trunk before he was back to holding me in his arms.

"I don't want ye to go," he said against my neck, and I felt my heart break in half at the sound of his voice. "Stay. Please, stay, Celeste."

"I can't," I said in response even though it wasn't at all the truth.

Like Tyra and I had talked about in our room, I could have stayed. There was absolutely nothing waiting for me at home. No mom. No job. No real obligations. Saying that I couldn't stay just felt like the right thing to do. It would be crazy of me to stay in another country with a man I barely knew.

Who in their right mind did something like that?

He pulled away from me and wiped the tears that had

started to fall from my cheeks. I looked at his face and did the same. It was odd, watching a grown man cry because his heart was breaking. Truth be told, it was sexy as hell even though I might have assumed the opposite before this moment.

"We'd better go," he said before looking away from me and reaching for his door handle.

I stepped outside, feeling unsteady on my own two feet. I'd never experienced anything like this before.

"We'll come back," Tyra said from behind the car, and I started nodding when Patrick was at my side again.

"I mean," I started, "we could come back."

"Okay," Patrick said, but I could tell that he didn't believe me. Not in the slightest. "Sure."

He knew that once we returned home and immersed ourselves in our own familiar worlds, we most likely wouldn't come back to Ireland. Our intentions were honorable now, but that all changed once you slipped back into your old routines and habits.

"I'll text you. And we can video-chat," I said, trying to sound hopeful, but I wasn't even sure why. What was I alluding to? Were we a couple now? Were we dating long distance?

"Ye bet your arse we'll video-chat. And text," Patrick said, surprising me.

We hadn't talked about this part of things. It'd seemed like both of us wanted to pretend it wasn't happening, so we'd put it off or ignored it altogether.

"Come on. We still have to go through security," Tyra said, suddenly sounding anxious to leave.

Before I could move to grab my suitcase, Patrick's hand stopped me. "I got ye something," he said before reaching into his pocket and pulling out a small silver ring.

I opened my hand, and he dropped it into my palm, where I grabbed it between my fingers and studied it. There was a crown on top of a heart, which was being held on each side by a set of hands.

"It's a claddagh ring," he said. "Originated here in Ireland." He started pointing at the parts of the ring as he explained it further. "The hands represent friendship. The heart represents love. And the crown represents loyalty."

It felt like a boulder had lodged itself in my throat. I couldn't breathe.

"It's beautiful," I squeaked out, managing to find the

words.

"Tradition says that the direction ye wear the heart shows if you're taken or not. If the heart points toward ye, your heart isn't available. But if it points outward, then you're single."

I turned the heart to point toward me as I slipped it on my ring finger on my right hand. "My heart is definitely not available," I said.

He picked me up in the air and held me tight as he kissed me hard, claiming me like he had the first night we were together. "I'm going to miss ye something fierce, my girl."

"Me too."

They walked us into the entrance, but we had to hurry through security, or we were going to be late.

"Text me the second ye land in America," he said, and I told him I would.

He grabbed me one last time and kissed me, his tongue sweeping in, touching mine, and my insides heated, wanting him.

And as his eyes started to water again, he turned away from me, grabbed Blaire, and disappeared out the glass doors.

"This sucks," Tyra said, and I threw my arm around her in agreement.

This definitely sucked.

I NEED HER

🍀

PATRICK

THE DRIVE BACK to Kilkenny was fecking brutal. My heart felt like it was in pieces inside my chest. It was a different kind of ache than when I'd lost my mum and my brother. This felt like I might never breathe right again. Like something inside me was now missing and was never coming back. Maybe it was a limb or a bone … something I could technically live without but would never be the same again after losing it.

"I'm a mess," Blaire said, interrupting my own pity party.

I knew that he and Tyra had connected as well, but of

course, I assumed that what they had couldn't even compare to the bond that Celeste and I had formed. It was an arsehole thing of me to think.

"Did you tell her to text you when she lands?" I asked.

"No," he said, and I looked at him like he'd fecked up already. "I told her to call."

"It'll be three in the morning here by the time they land," I said, hoping like hell I'd be able to sleep without her. I'd gotten used to having her body tucked up against mine.

"I know what time it will be. I don't care."

Maybe I should have told Celeste to call. I'd only asked her to text. I was an idiot. She was going to think that Blaire liked her sister more than I liked her.

"What are we gonna do?" he asked.

But I couldn't focus on Blaire and his feelings right now. I needed to get some kind of a handle on my own.

"We're gonna go back to the inn. You're going to fix the leaky faucet in room twelve and tighten the hinges on rooms four and two, and I'm going to check the books and make sure all the upcoming guests are situated and everyone is happy. And then we'll meet in the pub after."

"Yeah, or I might just head straight to the pub and drink

myself silly until you get there," he said before inhaling a long, loud breath.

"We've been lazy lately. We need to do our jobs," I said, putting on my boss voice. I hated using it and saying those things, but they were true.

We'd put things off to spend time with the girls, and while I wouldn't change it for anything, this was my business, my job, the way I made a living. We had to continue doing it right.

My phone vibrated, letting me know that I had a text message from the international app. I saw Celeste's name, and I couldn't press the button fast enough.

Miss you already. I love the ring. Thank you.

I loved her. I stopped myself from typing that back in response. Instead, I closed the app and continued driving, determined to text her when I could give her my full attention, which wasn't now.

We got back to the inn in record time, and the sounds of music were already spilling out of the pub's doors. It was still light out, but that never stopped anyone from having a good time. The instant I stepped out of my car and onto the dirt, I missed her even more. She had just been here, walking on this dirt, in the pub, behind the check-in counter.

A place that hadn't known her a week ago was now filled with memories of nothing but her. How had that happened so quickly? How could a stranger change the atmosphere of something I'd rebuilt without her in mind?

"I have to go to my place. I'll see ye later," I said toward Blaire, who was already walking in the direction of the pub before I stopped him. "Do your work first. Drink after," I insisted, and he rolled his eyes before saluting me like a soldier.

Stepping into my house, I was hit with a wave of emotions I hadn't expected. It almost bowled me right over. I saw her there, standing inside of my hearth, spinning around, a gorgeous smile on her face. She was everywhere. I feared that she always would be.

Pulling out my phone, I knew she was already in the air and most likely not on Wi-Fi, but I sent her a text anyway, so she would see it when she landed.

I CAN'T STOP THINKING ABOUT YE. I MISS YE SO MUCH THAT IT HURTS, SWEETHEART. COME BACK.

Before I could erase it or edit the message, I pressed Send. I hadn't been raised to be this emotionally open and honest. At least, not from my dad's perspective, but my mum had had far more of an influence over me than anyone else. I learned how to express myself and how to stay true to my heart. Which was how I found the strength to leave England and move to Ireland in the first place. My mum had raised me to live in my truth, no matter what anyone else said.

I spent the rest of the evening staring at my phone, waiting for her to land. After handling some minor issue with guests and making the rounds so that they felt welcome, I bailed on Blaire and went home instead of to the pub. I knew he was drowning his sorrows in whiskey. I simply wanted to toss my head in my pillow and breathe in the scent of her.

I must have fallen asleep because the sound of a text message woke me. My cell was lying next to me, and I grabbed it so fast, the brightness of the screen blinding my eyes. Turning it down, I pressed on the message.

Landed. Safe and sound. But have to admit, I hate being away from you.

My heart beat in triple time as I frantically typed out a response.

I'M GLAD YOU'RE SAFE. BUT I HATE THAT YOU'RE SO FAR AWAY.

The three dots appeared, and I knew that she was typing. I felt excited and exhilarated ... like a kid. No one had made me feel like this in years.

YOU'RE AWAKE! I HOPE I DIDN'T WAKE YOU. ACTUALLY, I KIND OF HOPE I DID. PATRICK ... I JUST ... MISS YOU. I MISS YOU SO MUCH ALREADY. IS THAT STUPID?

She attached a screenshot of what appeared to be her cell phone wallpaper. It was a picture of us at the Cliffs of Moher. I laughed because I'd already done the exact same thing, although I'd chosen a different photo. I snapped a screenshot of mine and sent it to her.

NOT STUPID. COME BACK. OR I'LL COME THERE AND BRING YE HOME.

LOL. NOT SURE I'D MIND THAT. GO TO SLEEP. TALK TOMORROW.

Even though I didn't want to let her go, I agreed, placing my phone on the charger and closing my eyes again.

When I reopened them, the light was streaming in through my window. It was a new day. One more where she still wasn't here.

※

IF I'D THOUGHT that things would get better with time, I was mistaken. Celeste and Tyra had been gone for ten days, and I swore to feck that I'd been aware of every single minute of all ten of those days. We texted on and off throughout the day and video-chatted at least once a day. Seeing her face fill my screen made my heart ache and swell at the same time.

Technology was a gift. It helped. But it didn't seem to ease what I truly wanted ... *her ... here ... with me.* That desire wasn't lessening. And Blaire was no longer my comrade in that regard.

I'd felt connected with him initially in our conjoined misery, but as time passed, Blaire missed Tyra less and less. And the same went for her, apparently. It wasn't that Blaire hadn't really liked Tyra. He had. But he saw a future together as an unrealistic option, and he let the thought of being with her go.

My thoughts refused to do the same. Being with Celeste hadn't felt unrealistic or impossible. It felt like something we could make happen if we both chose to. That wasn't saying that there wouldn't be challenges or that it wouldn't be hard, but it would be worth it. Because being together mattered more than being apart.

"I've never seen you so miserable." Blaire sidled up to me at the bar and took my drink for his own, finishing it off.

"I hate being here without her," I said, not caring what his response might be or if he'd make fun of me.

"I miss Tyra too, but …" He paused.

I realized that the way we missed the sisters wasn't the same, and we both knew it. Blaire missed Tyra because she was fun and silly and had brought a lot of laughter into his life, but I missed Celeste on a level that could only be described as soulful. She completed me, and as American as that sounded, it was the truth.

"I had to let her go. And you need to do the same," he pushed, and I felt myself getting angry.

I didn't like being told what to do or how to feel. Especially not when it came to my feelings or Celeste.

"There is no letting her go," I argued.

"There is if you just try. I mean"—he downed the rest of the drink before slapping my shoulder—"Tyra's going on a date later."

I practically choked on the air around us. "A date? And ye don't care?" I asked, knowing that if Celeste told me the same thing, I'd lose my damn mind, go to the airport, and get on a plane, just to fecking stop it from happening.

"Nah," he said like it was no big deal. "I have a date this weekend too. Tyra and I had fun while she was here, but now, she's not."

It really was that simple for him, and I couldn't begrudge him for it. I just had to walk my own path.

"I've got to go see her," I said point-blank.

"Yeah, I know," Blaire said with a smile that made his trademark dimples appear.

"Am I being a fool?" I asked, suddenly wondering what he did think.

"Only one way to find out."

I pushed up from the barstool and clapped him on the

back. "Guess I'm going to America."

"Come back with the lass or don't come back," he teased before wishing me good luck.

I'D KNOW THAT ACCENT ANYWHERE

♣

CELESTE

IT HAD BEEN almost two weeks since we'd been back from Ireland, and it still felt … *weird*. Nothing about being back in Dallas, in our childhood home, should have felt off, but it did, and I knew exactly why.

I didn't belong here anymore. In this place. Without him.

When I'd stepped onto the front porch and into our house, it was like stepping back in time somehow. And it had nothing to do with Mom and everything to do with me.

As I looked around at all of our things, noticing that nothing had changed in the days since we'd left, I knew that I would never be the same again. This trip had taken my being and shaken it up like a snow globe. All of my pieces were in new places, settled down differently. And I wasn't even mad about it; I just didn't know what to do.

Patrick and I talked every day, but neither one of us made plans to see the other or even brought the idea up. I had no clue what we were doing.

Do I have a boyfriend? Am I in a long-distance relationship with someone in another country?

It sure felt that way, but we never defined it or even tried to. I thought we were both scared. Especially after seeing how quickly whatever Tyra and Blaire had had slipped away into nothing. They both seemed fine with it, but if you had asked me a couple weeks ago, I would have sworn that they were just as into one another as Patrick and I were.

I would have been wrong. And that rattled me a little. Maybe with more time, Patrick and I would eventually stop talking too. Maybe whatever we had would fade off into the sunset, and I'd be left with nothing but my memories and pictures on my cell phone.

The thought pained my heart.

"Do you like my outfit?" Tyra suddenly appeared in the kitchen, dressed in new clothes from head to toe.

I'd told her about the money the day after we got back. I'd almost completely forgotten about it until she asked what we were going to do with our lives, going forward. She was talking about the house and whether or not we wanted to stay in Dallas. She'd liked living in Houston, and before Ireland, I'd always seen myself going back to Austin and teaching again.

Now, I had no idea what I wanted to do.

After I'd transferred her half of the money into her account, she'd danced around the house for a solid half hour, thanking Mom every two seconds in between twerks. We were so lucky that our mom had taken care of us so well. We'd both give it all back if it meant that she was still alive, but we knew that wasn't how life worked.

"You look gorgeous," I said as she twirled.

Tyra had no problem with spending the money. I'd yet to touch a penny of it.

"I have a date tonight."

I shook my head. I didn't disapprove of her dating; I was

just more in disbelief at how she could already. This was her third date this week.

"Don't shake your head at me," she chastised. "Blaire and I were fun. He was fun. And super hot in bed. But I live here and he lives there, and it is what it is."

If it was what it was, then how come I didn't even remotely feel the same way when it came to Patrick? I must have made some sort of face because Tyra was next to me at the kitchen table, a pout on her lips.

"Blaire and I had fun, Celeste," she repeated. "But it's not what you and Patrick have."

"What does that even mean? Am I supposed to up and move to Ireland?"

She shrugged. "Do you want to move to Ireland?" She was seriously asking me. She wasn't being condescending or judgmental in any way.

"I really loved it there," I said, reminiscing about how peaceful and calm I'd felt, just being on that land. Twisting the ring that was still on my finger, I stared at it, remembering the moment he had given it to me and asked me to choose the direction I placed the heart.

"Home doesn't feel like home anymore, does it?" She

pressed her lips together as she waited for me to respond, but I could tell she already knew the answer.

I couldn't really say the words out loud, so I slowly shook my head instead right as the doorbell rang.

"Is that your date already?" I looked up at the clock on the wall. It was only afternoon.

"No. I'll get it." She hopped up from the chair and skipped to the door before pulling it open.

I strained my neck to see who it was without moving from my spot when my body grew painfully still. My mind started racing, my heart stopped beating, and my throat grew so thick that I thought it might have closed up entirely.

A man's voice saying words I couldn't quite make out, but that didn't matter.

I knew that accent.

I'd know it anywhere.

But how was it … here? Outside my mom's front door?

"Uh, Celeste? You're going to want to get this," Tyra screamed before she ran back into the kitchen and helped me to my feet.

I rounded the corner and stepped into the living room, where Patrick stood, his hands in front of his body, his eyes looking tired from the travel.

"What are you doing here?" I asked. It wasn't the best way to greet the man I couldn't picture my life without, but it was the first words I could find.

His green eyes met mine and held them. "I can't stop thinking about you. I miss you so damn much." His voice broke as he said the words. Like maybe he was just now realizing the risk he had taken in coming here. What if I denied him? Or told him I wanted him to go?

"I miss you too," I said before launching into his arms and melting against his chest.

God, I'd missed the way his body felt around mine more than I knew.

"I can't believe you're here," Tyra squealed before looking around him, possibly thinking that Blaire was somewhere behind him.

"He didn't come," Patrick said, and I swore her eyes flashed with hurt for only a second before she tucked it away and pretended like it didn't matter.

"What are you doing here? Patrick, the inn …" I started to think of all the things he'd left behind to be here right now, and I still had no idea why he'd come.

"The inn's in good hands. It can survive without us for a little bit," he said, and I didn't miss the use of the word *us*.

"Us?" I questioned.

"Come back with me, Celeste. Come home to Ireland and be with me."

How can I do that? Is it fair of him to ask me to uproot my whole life and move there when he hadn't even offered to do the same for me?

"You could move here," I suggested, knowing that it wasn't even remotely realistic.

I was being stubborn. Fighting for independence that I didn't need.

He had a business there. Obligations. And I ... I had nothing here anymore, except Tyra.

"I could do that, aye," he started to say, as if he was willing to give it all up for me. As if being with me was more important than everything else.

"You'd do that?"

"If that's what ye want, aye." He gulped as he stepped toward me, taking my hands in his own, letting me know that he meant every word that he said.

"But ... you'd be giving up more than I would," I

admitted. "You have things that you built there. And I …" My eyes started to water. "What would I do in Ireland?"

"Help me run the inn? Challenge Americans to drinking contests? Anything ye want, sweetheart. Just please come back with me. I can't live the rest of my life without ye. I mean, I suppose that I could, but I don't want to. Please tell me ye feel the same."

"Of course she feels the same," Tyra shouted from somewhere in the house, and I started laughing, knowing that she had been eavesdropping. She stepped out of the shadows and into the living room, where we still stood, holding hands. "She's been miserable since we came back. I don't know why she won't come out and say it."

"Is that true?" He looked at me, his eyes imploring, begging to hear my truth.

"It's true," I admitted.

"I can't go back to Ireland without ye. You've ruined it for me."

I laughed again, wiping at the tears that started falling. It was one hundred percent batshit crazy of me to say yes to Patrick, but I said yes anyway. It wasn't like I would be stuck in Ireland if I hated it or if we didn't work out for some reason. But something told me that we would be just fine.

"I want to go back with you."

Tyra jumped up and down like a lunatic, and I looked at her.

"Are you sure you'll be okay if I leave? It's not like I'll only be a couple hours away."

"You're crazy if you think you're moving there without me. I mean," she started, waving her fingers around, "I'm not *moving there*, moving there, but I want a room. A place I can stay for as long as I want, as often as I want." She spoke very matter-of-factly, like she'd thought about this before today. "I think I'll go back and forth between there and here."

I looked up at Patrick, wondering if that was okay with him or not, and he started laughing.

"You and Blaire are going to give me heart palpitations," was all he said, and Tyra shrugged like he could handle it.

"Think he'll be upset if I show up too?"

"No. He likes ye. He just didn't think ye two had a future, so …"

"Yeah, yeah. I know. He'd better not have a girlfriend

whenever I come to visit." She turned on her heels and stomped down the hallway.

"Are there things ye need to wrap up here? Can ye move, just like that?" he asked, snapping his fingers, and I nodded.

"Honestly? Everything's taken care of. And I suppose I could handle whatever isn't online. We don't have anything, except for this house, and it's all paid for."

"How soon can ye pack?" He kissed my lips and brought my body back to life.

I'd been in some sort of waking coma since I'd been back in Dallas, but just one kiss from him shook me from it all.

He was the Prince Charming in my fairy tale.

EPILOGUE

♣

CELESTE

EIGHT MONTHS LATER

FROM OUR LIVING room window, I stared out at my fiancé, who was greeting the new incoming guests in front of the inn.

Just the other night, Patrick had proposed to me in front of everyone in the pub.

We were eating dinner in the same booth where we had the first night we met. The place was packed to the gills, musicians playing, people dancing, Tyra and Blaire annoyingly flirting with one another ... again.

When the music suddenly stopped and every single

person in the pub looked our way, I swore I might have a breakdown. I had no idea what was going on, and then Patrick stepped out of the booth and dropped to one knee. He had everyone in on it. They'd all known he was going to ask, and I had been sitting there, wholly unaware.

There was no way I was saying no.

And I didn't. I practically dived headfirst into his waiting arms as he slipped the green emerald on my left hand. It was the ring I'd fallen in love with at one of the local stores downtown. I didn't even think he was paying attention to my gawking and fawning. Apparently, he had been.

"It's the one ye wanted, aye?" he asked as my eyes spilled over with happy tears, and everyone started cheering and hollering so loud that I could barely hear my fiancé talking to me over the noise.

"Yes. It's stunning," I said as I admired it on my hand.

I wondered if I'd ever get tired of seeing it there, and then I knew that I wouldn't.

"I can't believe I get to marry you!" I shouted, and he kissed me like no one else was in the room.

Tyra sprinted over toward us with a grin so big on her face that it made me giggle. "Let me see." She reached for my hand and pulled it close to her face. "It was beautiful in the box, but it's even prettier on your hand."

She turned to look for Blaire, who was standing right behind her, his hand on her waist. "That's a good ring, don't you think? Not simple, like a diamond. Everyone gets a diamond. Take notes, B."

Blaire looked like he might throw up, but he hid it well from everyone, except me.

I'd gotten to know him really well these past eight months. Aside from Patrick, he was my closest friend and the person I spent the most time with. He really did like my sister, but he said she gave him whiplash with the way her heart changed. I knew he was just trying to protect his.

Tyra kept coming out here, her visits growing longer each time. I wondered how long it would be until she moved here completely even though she kept insisting that she would never leave our home in Dallas. At least, not entirely. She'd even convinced Blaire to go out there with her when she left this time, just to see how he liked it.

They were going to end up together. I'd put money on it. But the real question was, where would they end up?

Here … or there?

My fiancé walked toward our house, spotting me in the window, his face breaking out in a genuine smile. God, he was something to look at. And he was all mine.

"Where's my future wife?" he asked as he stepped through the door, and I gave him a look that told him to come and get me just as I started stripping off my clothes. "Oh, sweetheart. Are we playing that game?"

I dropped my shirt to the ground as I headed toward our bedroom, followed by my yoga pants as I stepped out of them.

I heard him behind me, picking up the discarded items, like he always did whenever I teased him this way. By the time I reached the bed, I was completely naked, and my man was basically foaming at the mouth.

"God, you're stunning. My future wife. My fiancée. The love of my life," he said, getting himself undressed as fast as possible.

He was on top of me before I could inhale another breath, his mouth hot, his tongue wet as he kissed me like I belonged to him even though we both knew that I did.

It worked both ways. He belonged to me too. And that

would never change.

I was never moving away from Ireland for as long as I lived. To be honest, I didn't miss being home in America. I'd found somewhere new to call home. With a man I couldn't have found back in Dallas. This kind of man simply didn't exist there.

I knew my mom was looking down on me with joy—hopefully not in this particular moment, but regardless. I thought she had known exactly what she was doing when she set this trip up. At least, I liked to think so.

THE END ☘

Thank You

Thank you so much for reading Patrick and Celeste's story. I hope you enjoyed the trip through Ireland as much as I enjoyed writing it! I had so much fun, you guys! I came up with the idea for my Fun for the Holiday's Collection to give you lighthearted, happy reads that you could get lost in. I know that the world has been crazy lately, hopefully this helped you escape… if only for a little while. <3

About the Author

Jenn Sterling is a Southern California native who loves writing stories from the heart. Every story she tells has pieces of her truth in it as well as her life experience. She has her bachelor's degree in radio/TV/film and has worked in the entertainment industry the majority of her life.

Jenn loves hearing from her readers and can be found online at:

Blog & Website:
www.j-sterling.com

Twitter:
www.twitter.com/AuthorJSterling

Facebook:
www.facebook.com/AuthorJSterling

Instagram:
@AuthorJSterling